# Contents

i

# The Greek Constellations – Gemini

# *The Greek Constellations – Gemini*

**Stephan De Jonghe**

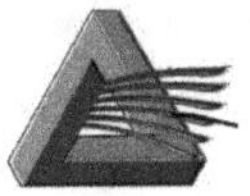

# *Copyright*

**The Greek Constellations – Gemini**
**Copyright © 2024 by Stephan De Jonghe**



*The characters and events described in this book are based on personal research from numerous references. Any resemblance to actual persons, or events is purely coincidental.*

For permission requests, write to the publisher at: stephansfolliclefarm@gmail.com

Ordering Information:

Special discounts are available on quantity purchases by book resellers, corporations, associations, and others. For details, contact the publisher at the email address above.

**The Greek Constellations – Gemini, by Stephan De Jonghe**

International
ISBN 978-1-7636516-0-9 (paperback)
ISBN 978-1-7636516-1-6 (e-book)
USA
ISBN 1-7636516-0-6 (paperback)
ISBN 1-7636516-1-4 (e-book)

Publisher
Stephan De Jonghe Publishing,
Hillarys, Perth, Western Australia, Australia 6025

Printer and distributor
Ingram Content Group
1 Ingram Blvd.
La Vergne, Tennessee USA 37086

1

# *Cover*


*In the footsteps of Homer and Hesiod.*


**From Astronomy to Mythology**


**How the constellations came to be named by the Greek God's.**


**Stephan De Jonghe**


**Novella Nine**
**The constellation**
**Gemini**


**The story of the twins Castor and Polydeuces, and the constellation Cygnus or "The Swan."**

2

# *The dedication*

To say that my darling wife is the love of my life is an understatement. Deb is my best friend, soul mate, confidant, and life partner.

Among so many other things, we also share a love of books, and we have a massive library on display in our home of books that we want to read.

Our topics include action, comedy, romance, science fiction, crime, thrillers, and adventure. We also have an impressive non-fiction collection.

My endeavours as an author represent a passion that burns powerfully for me. I am driven to write.

I have many stories to tell, and writing them and publishing them is my way of contributing to other people's library's.

Writing involves many hours of research and then sitting in solitude, slowly assembling the words that details a journey into a readable story. One that was only previously an idea.

This takes a lot of patience and persistence.

After the story is put down, the process of editing begins. Few non-writers understand that this stage can take as much five times longer than it takes to write the actual first draft.

My Deb gives me the support that I need to execute my writing passion. She not only supports my writing, but also enjoys reading the stories.

Her assistance with proof reading, feed-back on content, and editing, is invaluable. Especially after I've become blind to my own errors. She understands how important it is to me and to you, the reader, to get it right.

I dedicate these books to my wife as my thanks to her for her on-going support, and for her contributions to the finished publications. We are a team.

We both hope that you enjoy this series of books, and we look forward to your feedback.

Stephan and Deb De Jonghe

**3**

# *Special thanks to Janey Emery*

My special thanks go to Janey Emery – A renowned artist, for giving me permission to use her art for the covers for my Greek Constellation series of books.

I hope you enjoy her art and the story within these pages.
Stephan De Jonghe - Author

**Janey's Story** - Born in Narrogin, Western Australia, Janey Emery's interest in art began as early as 2 years of age and led to art becoming the central element in Janey's Childhood. Excelling in art throughout her school years Janey devoted herself to the art course provided by Balcatta Senior High school, where her passion for art only intensified.

Janey has been painting full-time since 1991 and has attained a high degree of respect in the art world from peers and art lovers alike. Janey has won numerous distinguished artistic awards for her work and has sold many paintings throughout Australia and overseas. Janey

Emery is achieving the recognition her distinctive artistic talents deserve.

Janey is Self-Taught in All Mediums with the exception of leisure courses undertaken in Oil and Water Colours.

Janey specialises in paintings of the magnificent Karri tree forests of the South West region of Western Australia

*Art has always played a part of who I am. From early childhood to now there has been a need for me to express myself through drawing and painting. I find peace in my craft, and I hope I bring that to my paintings. To me, my Art is like breathing. Painting is my life.*

*Janey Emery*
https://www.janeyemery.art/

# *Authors note*

*T*his story is based on Greek mythology. The word Gemini however, is Latin for "twins". Many thousands of years ago, the origin of the constellation Gemini was one of the stories imagined by ancient travellers and sailors. Also included in this book is the story of the constellation Cygnus, or "the Swan."

Many of these stories owe some of their earlier history to the Phoenicians, Babylonians, and Mycenaean's, and were initially used to help ancient travellers remember star patterns as a nighttime navigational tool. Over time, these fascinating stories were greatly embellished on how the constellations came to be formed. The ancient Greeks called these constellations the "Katasterismoi" meaning, "the placing of the stars." They gave names and told stories about forty-eight out of the eighty-eight constellations that are recognised by the International Astronomical Union.

These mythologies were embellished as they were countlessly re-told with tales of gods encountering wild creatures, fighting fierce battles, and of course having lots of sex. After all, these men were away from home for lengthy periods of time. They shared these stories to entertain urban dwellers that they encountered, and from there the stories became legends, and for many people they became their religion.

*A Greek poet and storyteller named Homer, was the first person to document these stories and he is most famous for the "Iliad" and the "Odyssey" which he composed some 2,800 years ago. Whilst very little is known about Homer, he is regarded by many as the founder of modern literature. His two main works were the first literary works to be taught formally to students. Interestingly, there are thirty-three film adaptations of the Odyssey, proving his works are still relevant to modern audiences.*

*Later, a poet named Hesiod, significantly contributed to Greek mythology and followed on from Homer's work. Together they are attributed with establishing ancient Greek religious customs, formal astronomy, the development of structured learning, documenting events, early economics, commercial farming, and time keeping.*

*The word "zodiac" originated from the Greek words "Zodiakos kuklos," meaning "circle of little animals". It wasn't until 50BCE that the first classical zodiac depicting the twelve astrological star signs in their current order was first depicted. It is known as the "Dendera zodiac."*

*During the $2^{nd}$ century CE, a Greco-Roman astrologer and astronomer named Claudius Ptolemy worked on his documented Tetrabiblos into what is regarded as western astrology's primary source document and remains largely in use today. Also of note is that astronomers have named a crater on the Luna surface, and another on the surface of the planet Mars Ptolemaeus, in honour of Ptolemy and his contribution to astronomy.*

*The connection between Greek names and Roman names for the same deities came from their translation from one language to the other. In ancient Greek, Zeus is pronounced Dias. In Latin that became Djous Pater (Sky father) or Luppiter. In English this became Jupiter. Many names evolved in this way.*

*As an author, my goal is to turn what is known of the mythology, into an enjoyable story for today's reader.          Stephan J De Jonghe*

**5**

# *Chronology*

Yet another note from the author,

My "from astronomy to mythology" series of novellas posed some difficulties in terms of writing the stories into a logical chronology. Until the Iliad, and the Odyssey, no one had ever written any of the tales of titan's forming the world, or their ultimate defeat by the gods who eventually resided in Mount Olympus. These stories were imagined piecemeal, embellished, refined, and retold over a thousand-year period. Unlike history, which did happen on a linear timeline and can be plotted, the timeline used in fictional stories were not relevant, and by their very nature at the whim of the story teller. Over the millennia, re-tellers of the stories frequently added details, and characters that were often inconsistent with the other stories. No one knew and no one cared, as they were mostly just for entertainment.

For the more serious devotees, these stories were the basis for a religion, and many aspects of the stories were used to focus worshippers' attention, and they were therefore treated by many at the time as historical facts. They focused their attention on those gods and goddesses that were consistent with their beliefs and values.

The best example that I can use to demonstrate the challenge of chronology, is referencing a main character known as Pandora. As she is the first human woman, she features in her own story, but she was created by Hephaestus, the son of Zeus and Hera, and it happened when Zeus and Hera were already married. But Zeus met and fell in love with Europa, a human woman, who was alive before he married Hera, and before he had a son to ask to make the first woman. Challenging!

As an author with a particular attention to detail, (at least I believe I do), the chronology of Greek mythological events became increasing important to me as the list of novellas planned for this series grew to thirteen.

I have therefore prepared a simple chronology (that may or may not be consistent with other writers of this genre) to assist readers in sorting out the sequence of events that occur in the stories that I am sharing with you. (Spoiler alert!)

I now believe that Greek Mythology Chronology should be a legitimised field of study all on its own. (Perhaps it already is?)

<u>The novella.</u>      <u>The details of the event.</u>
<u>(the subject of ongoing revision)</u>

| | |
|---|---|
| Pisces | Gaia forms the earth, oceans and skies. She is the earth mother. |
| Pisces | Gaia gives birth to Uranus. |
| Pisces | Cronus is born and defeats Uranus when released from confinement. |
| Pisces | Aphrodite is born. |
| Capricorn | Pricus is the father of the sea-goats. |
| Pisces | Cronus is crowned king and marries Rea. Zeus is one of their six children. |

| | |
|---|---|
| Centaurus | Cronus mates with Philyra. Chiron is born. |
| Pandora | Prometheus creates a race of human men - The golden age. |
| Pandora | Prometheus creates a second race of human men - The silver age. |
| Pandora | Prometheus creates a third race of human men - The bronze age. |
| Pisces | Zeus defeats Cronus and Zeus is crowned King of the Gods. |
| Pisces | Zeus marries Metis, Athena is born, but Metis dies. |
| Pisces | Zeus marries but then quickly divorces Themis. |
| Pandora | Prometheus creates a fourth race of human men - The iron age. |
| Sagittarius | Crotus invents the bow and arrow. |
| Pisces | Zeus marries Hera. Ares, Eileithyia, Hephaestus, and Hebe are born. |
| Pisces | Aphrodite arrives at Mount Olympus and marries Hephaestus. |
| Pandora | Hephaestus creates Pandora as the first human woman. |
| Taurus | Zeus meets Europa. |
| Scorpio | Zeus mates with Leto. Apollo and Artemis are born. |
| Scorpio | Poseidon mates with Euryale. Orion is born. |
| Scorpio | Atalanta is recused as an infant and now runs with Artemis. |
| Aries | Zeus creates a cloud nymph and names her Nephele. |
| Aries | Poseidon mates with Theophane. Chrysomallos is born. |

| | |
|---|---|
| Aries | Nephele marries Athamas. The twins, Helle and Phrixus are born. |
| Aries | Chrysomallos rescues Helle and Prixus. |
| Ophiuchus | Apollo mates with Coronis. Asclepius is born. |
| Cancer/Leo | Zeus mates with Alkmene. Herakles is born. |
| Gemini | Zeus mates with Leda. Polydeuces and Castor are born. |
| Pisces | Aphrodite mates with Ares. Eros is born. |
| Scorpio | Orion meets and befriends Hephaistos. |
| Virgo/Libra | Zeus visits Themis and Astraea. |
| Cancer/Leo | Herakles is assigned the first of his ten labours. |
| Cancer/Leo | Herakles befriends Chiron. |
| Centaurus | Chiron befriends Herakles. |
| Gemini | Castor and Polydeuces join the Argo crew. |
| Cancer/Leo | Herakles joins Argo crew. |
| Gemini | Atalanta asks to join Argo crew. |
| Scorpio | Orion meets Artemis. |
| Centaurus | Chiron commences formally as a teacher. |
| Gemini | Herakles is inadvertently separated from the Argo. |
| Cancer/Leo | Herakles resumes his labours. |
| Scorpio | Orion duels with the giant scorpion. |
| Gemini | Jason and Argo crew return with the Golden Fleece. |
| Gemini | Calydonian Boar Hunt. |
| Gemini | Atalanta joins the Calydonian Boar Hunt. |
| Cancer/Leo | Herakles accidently wounds Chiron. |
| Centaurus | Chiron makes his plea to Zeus. |

| | |
|---|---|
| Pisces | The Greeks and the Trojans start a war that lasts ten years. |
| Aquarius | Zeus meets Ganymede. |
| Cancer/Leo | Herakles becomes immortal and marries Hebe. |
| Pisces | Atalanta competes in a running race against her potential suitors. |
| Gemini | Castor and Polydeuces become immortal. |
| Pisces | Aphrodite and Eros escape Typhon. |

Stephan De Jonghe

## 6

# *The Story of Gemini*

This story, like so many in Greek mythologies, starts with Zeus having sex with an innocent mortal woman and that their tryst resulted in the birth of a demi-god. Zeus' had a lengthy history of passionate liaisons with beautiful, often naive, young women who were cunningly manipulated into willingly copulating with him. Naturally, the stories boasted that the sex was amazing...

Leda's mother, Leucippe, was so enthusiastic about the prospect of becoming a grandmother, that she actively encouraged her daughter Leda to increase her sexual frequency with her husband, Tyndareus, the King of the Spartans. Leda desperately wanted children and she also adored her mother and so didn't want to disappoint her. She frequently initiated couplings with her husband in order to conceive children. Tyndareus also wanted children and he really enjoyed the sex, so he offered absolutely no resistance to performing his manly contribution when invited.  To everyone's amusement, he quickly became aroused whenever he was summoned by his wife. When this happened during important meetings, he'd blush, mumble an apology, and bluster out of the room.

But, despite their undying love, fervent passion, and frequent lovemaking, Leda didn't become pregnant. Leucippe was disappointed and became despondent with the lack of progress in the pro-creation of grandchildren, so she did what any desperate grandmother would do; she requested divine assistance from the gods. She went straight to the top, to the king of all their gods, Zeus, with a message of her daughter's, and her own, urgent plight.

Zeus, on learning that a desirable woman needed him, became immediately intrigued. He didn't like to disappoint, or waste an opportunity. While his wife, Hera, was distracted with her teachings of morality and fidelity to mortals, he thought he'd visit Leda and possibly, hopefully, give Hera something new to talk about.

Leucippe prayed in a temple that had been erected in Zeus' honour. She knew that Zeus had fathered more children than the Greek mortals could remember, so he'd know a thing or two about the best way for Leda to become pregnant. As she boldly sung out Zeus' praises, Zeus returned the compliment by materialising before her. He then graciously thanked her for the invitation. Leucippe was at first overjoyed to see him, but then she became concerned.

'Do you plan to bed my daughter?' she challenged.

'Only if she'd like me to...' Zeus replied with a boyish grin. Despite many women hesitating, or even offering token resistance, he'd actually experienced minimal refusals.

'Leda has love only for Tyndareus.' Leucippe cautioned.

'And she should continue to stay that way,' Zeus replied calmly. 'I have no desire to form a relationship with your daughter,' he promised her as he smiled.

'So, you'll favour her with pregnancy?' Leucippe was now more hopeful.

'I'll see to it personally,' Zeus reassured the old woman.

'She will not grant you an audience.' Leucippe was now concerned about how his godly assistance would impact on Leda. 'Perhaps you'll have to enrich Tyndareus' seed so that he can produce children.'

Zeus could do that, but it would deny him the physical pleasure he so enjoyed and was now looking forward to having. He had travelled a long way from Mount Olympus, and he was feeling the excitement about having sex with someone new. Why should this mortal King of Sparta have all the fun? He looked at Leucippe and smiled. 'I'm confident that can be arranged.'

Zeus then appeared to vanish before Leucippe's eyes, but he had turned himself into vapour and then slowly drifted away. He drifted closer to the grounds surrounding the house in search of Leda. He reformed behind a structure and watched the activity with interest. He observed that there were numerous geese, swans, chickens, and ducks, roaming this part of the Tyndareus gardens. These birds were a replenishing food source and would provide meals to the many residents, their staff, and the numerous visitors to the royal family. Birds, pigs, sheep, and cattle, were often kept in close proximity to the kitchens. He then spied a gorgeous nubile woman who he believed to be Leda. It was obvious that it was her for she wore the typical robes of a noble Spartan queen and had a retinue of staff to do her bidding.

It was Leda's habit to personally attend the swans. She felt they were regal birds and were therefore given better feed and had more liberties than other farm animals. Their slaughter and consumption were reserved for special occasions, which were rare, and so she had the opportunity to become quite attached to many of them. When Leda headed towards the flock of swans, they immediately recognised her and screeched in delight at her approach.

Leda had her hands full of feed and treats that the swans enjoyed, and her assistants knew to keep away, so as to give their queen the fun she so much looked forward to having. Zeus spied his opportunity. He morphed into a swan and waddled over to them and joined the bevy in the effort to gain her attention. The swans were soon sated and began to relax. Leda sought out her regular place to sit and enjoy their company. As she sat, Zeus still disguised as a swan, stepped up to her and laid his head on her lap. Leda was delighted as this was a first, and so she contentedly stroked the swans' neck becoming very happy and relaxed.

The swan next lifted its head and looked nervously about. Leda was amused and reassured the bird with loving tones. 'It's okay my sweet. You are safe with me,' she assured the swan as she stroked it some more.

When Zeus the swan, was satisfied that there were no humans in the vicinity, he transformed once more into his human form. Naked, he sat confidently beside her, sporting his famously generous, but at the same time mischievous, grin.

'Oh! Are you, Zeus?' Leda was startled at the transformation and in total awe of their favoured God.

'I am,' he replied. 'Your mother invited me to visit with you,' he told her as he danced his bushy eyebrows playfully, whilst maintaining his reassuring smile. Zeus' face portrayed the anticipation of mutual pleasure and satisfaction.

'My mother?' Leda was confused.

'She contacted me and explained that you wanted to have a baby. She knows that I have had much experience and skills in achieving that for you,' Zeus promised her smiling benevolently.

'But,' she paused considering Zeus' reputation. 'I love my husband, and we're both trying….' She was bewildered by her mother's interference, and overwhelmed by Zeus' presence.

'And so, you should. You both want children and so I'm here to help the two of you.'

'Oh!' She looked into his face and he seemed so sincere. 'Thank you,' she said, and fell into his arms in a gratifying embrace.

Zeus took this as his cue and became quickly aroused. Leda felt the giant member growing next to her body and suddenly became aware that Zeus intended to impregnate her personally.

'Oh,' she said and quickly moved away from him in concern.

'You like?' he said indicating his engorged member.

Zeus wasn't a god to offend, so she didn't. 'It's… magnificent,' she said praising him.

He drew her closer and kissed her fully on the lips. She trembled, frightened, but also at the same time finding herself surrendering to the moment. His strong arms lifted her easily, and she found herself being manoeuvred into a position where she was straddling him where he sat. He entered her comfortably, and within seconds she was lost in rapturous waves of pleasure. She found herself increasing her own rhythmic pelvic thrusts, pushing him deeper inside of her. He held her buttocks assisting her movements and she soon climaxed, whimpering happily at the extreme pleasure she was feeling. He remained firm deep inside of her, so she gently rode him, glowing in the simmering lingering ecstasy of him. These movements soon rekindled her euphoric feelings, and once again she intensely climaxed. She was exhausted and so rested her body against his. She whispered into his ear. 'It must be your turn,' she invited.

Zeus obliged and despite her weight on his lap he effortlessly commenced his thrusts into her. His own climax produced a third orgasm for Leda, and she was feeling faint and exhausted. They were both spent and so they relaxed. He looked her in the face and smiled. 'It is done,' he informed her, nodding happily. 'You are now with child.'

Leda was happy but conflicted at the same time. The fact that Zeus knew she was pregnant wasn't a surprise for her, as he was a god and he would know these things. The reality that she was finally pregnant was joyous news, but she was concerned about how she would explain what happened to her husband. She dismounted him and arranged her clothing.

Zeus stood and smiled as he bowed. He really enjoyed providing this type of service. He also knew all about discretion, and so he transformed back into a swan and waddled back to join the other swans, greedily pecking at random food scraps, as he felt hungry. When he saw his chance, he wandered over to the stone wall, passed through a gap, and headed for the trees. There, he transformed once more into an eagle form and leapt into the sky. Zeus was happy about being of assistance in making the baby and decided he would show an interest in the infants' future. He unhurriedly flew back to his home at Mount Olympus.

Later that night, as he lay naked but alone on his bed, he replayed his recent adventure in his mind. He decided that his visit with Leda was going to become a memorable encounter. She was both willing and pleased with the outcome. He recalled the fun of being a swan, which was a first for him. He rolled off the bed and stood and walked out onto his balcony gazing up at the night sky and pointed. 'There,' he said, and for the first time ever, the constellation "Cygnus" or better known as "The Swan" appeared in the starlit sky.

***

Leda sought out her mother for an explanation, and also to share the exciting news of her forthcoming child. She found her mother in her chambers. 'Mother, did you invite Zeus?' She was careful not to sound hostile. They had a close and loving mother daughter relationship, which both of them valued and preserved.

'I did.' She found it difficult to gauge if she were in trouble with her daughter.

'Well, he has visited me,' Leda told her.

'He said he would. I'm sorry. I should have warned you of my intentions, but when I prayed to him, he surprised me by actually showing up. You know we pray to the gods all the time for all sorts of things and, well, I never expected him to actually come here in person.'

'And you told him that I wanted to have a baby?' Leda wasn't angry with her mother. Her intentions were good, and she was with child, after all.

'Yes.' She confirmed with some hesitation.

'Well, it worked. Zeus came to me disguised as a swan. He was so cute and I stroked him. He suddenly transformed into his normal form and the next thing I knew he was inside of me sowing his seed.'

'He raped you?' Leda was suddenly alarmed.

'No!' Leda defended. 'It was wonderful,' she sighed. 'I climaxed three times and that never…' her voice trailed off. They were close, but this may have been too much information for her mother.

'Leda. Listen to your mother. If anyone asks, you were raped. Tyndareus would never understand that you gave yourself willingly to another man, even a god, and even worse that you enjoyed it.'

'How do I explain to him about our baby?' Leda rubbed her abdomen.

'You must copulate with him now, today. Then he'll only ever believe that the child is his.' Leucippe advised.

Leda nodded her agreement. She summonsed up the courage to find her husband and engage him in a sexual union. She felt guilty and had little desire to copulate so soon, but knew that her mother was right and that she must receive her husband's seed to assure him that he was the father of the baby.

She found Tyndareus in council with his advisors. She gave him that knowing look. The others knew full well what she wanted, it was common knowledge and they were respectful enough not to smile or acknowledge her summoning of her husband for sexual activity. Also, they knew the importance of producing an heir. Tyndareus excused himself, followed his wife into their bed chamber, disrobed and mounted her. She was puzzled by his lack of enthusiasm but laid back and moaned softly as if in pleasure. He came predictably as he always did. She decided to find out what was wrong.

'You didn't seem pleased to be with me?' She looked thoughtfully into his eyes trying to detect the feelings within them.

'You were seen in the swan garden with another man. He swore to me that you mounted him and then sent him away.' He spoke with an even tone, not angry or upset, just repeating what he'd been told.

She was immediately sorry. 'The man was Zeus. He forced himself on me after disguising himself as a swan.'

Tyndareus thought about this for a while. The same sort of thing had happened to his close friend Amphitryon, King of the Tiryns. He had felt sorry for him at the time, and now this was happening to him also. He too felt helpless against the might of the most powerful god.

'I believe you,' he said, but he wasn't smiling. He wasn't happy about their god's apparent transgression. It was just that he wanted to get a clear picture of the events in his mind. He loved his wife, and he believed that she truly loved him also. He didn't want to lose all that they had together. 'I suppose your mother invited him?' he asked, but still he wasn't angry.

'Yes, but she didn't expect him to actually come here to help us. She just wanted our love to produce grandchildren for her,' she explained. 'She's desperate.' Leda moved closer to hug and comfort her husband. These events were stressful to both of them.

Tyndareus guffawed. Leda began to laugh also, but more in relief from the tension release, than enjoying the ironic humour. When they settled, they relaxed once more into each other's arms.

'So, I gather we are with child?' he felt her stiffen next to him.

'Yes,' she answered meekly.

'So, having sex with me just now was to confuse who the actual father is,' he concluded.

'My mother suggested it.'

'Did you enjoy it?'

'I love you, so I always enjoy our love making.'

'I meant with him.'

'Oh.' She hesitated. She didn't want to lie, but she didn't want to share the truth of her climaxes. 'He's a god. I felt powerless, like I had lost all control of what he was doing to me. It wasn't rape, as he did do it with kindness, but I felt I couldn't prevent what was happening to me. When he told me that I was pregnant, I was happy, but also sad, because I want this to be your baby.'

He sat upright in bed and held her arms in his powerful hands. 'I promise you that I will love the child as my own,' he assured her and then he felt his wife relax. He smiled reassuringly and knew she would be relieved of his acceptance. Now that they had shared the details of what happened and were both resolved to accept them, they could continue to live their happy life together.

***

The pregnancy resulted in a big belly for Leda. The Spartans were over joyed at the news that their King and Queen were finally having their baby. As her pregnancy progressed, her mother and the attendant midwife, was convinced that there was more than one child in Leda's tummy; such was the size of her. Leda commented on several occasions about the wrestling and jostling in her belly that felt like a whole tribe fighting it out for any available space in her womb.

She walked about their home with difficulty and she needed frequent rests. Tyndareus wasn't surprised as the same thing had happened several years earlier to Alkmene, wife of King Amphitryon, when Zeus had also impregnated her.

Zeus was always quick to boast to anyone that his seed was powerful stuff. In this case, when his combined with Tyndareus' seed within his wife's womb, it made all the sperm exceptionally powerful. On the day of the birth, the family were surprised that Leda gave birth to four babies. She had delivered two boys and two girls. Leda didn't suffer excessively through the delivery. There was some consternation that Hera, displeased with her husband's infidelity, might have caused problems for Leda, but their births were relatively normal, and her pain and effort during the birthing process were what was anticipated. Leda and her babies were healthy and strong. Leda was especially relieved and looked forward to walking as a normal person once more.

In ancient Greek times, twins were often thought off as a curse on a family. Twins were rare and therefore their arrival aroused suspicions of infidelity, or that the mother was being punished by Hera, or some other vindictive goddess. At best, the parents of twins would be troubled both financially, and mentally, with the raising of two babies. At worst they could become alienated from other Greek families.

Triplets almost never happened, and the mother often died during childbirth. Quadruplets were therefore completely unimaginable. Tyndareus and Leda quickly decided that they didn't have four babies, but instead they had two sets of twins. Their home was big, and their staffing numbers were sufficient so that they'd cope. They named the sons, Castor and Polydeuces and daughters, Helen and Clytemnestra.

During a meeting of the immediate family, and the trusted staff members that attended them, they decided that they would invent wild tales in explanation of the four babies. One was told to describe the lengthy process of selecting and adopting worthy orphans. Another person would talk about the arrival of the babies hatched from a basket of eggs left to them by the Gods. Yet another would talk about the four babies coming to the family in a giant decorative box filled with precious gifts and golden trinkets. In this way, the conflicting stories would blur and confuse outsiders interest levels. Hopefully, the family would be left in peace to raise their children.

As the babies grew into children, their parents agreed that Polydeuces and Helen were conceived from Zeus' seed. Both Castor and Clytemnestra bore such a close family resemblance to Tyndareus that they both concluded that they were from his.

Leda was both delighted and secretly relieved, when her husband kept his promise and loved all of the four children deeply and equally. There union remained a happy one, and over the years, she and Tyndareus had three more baby girls. They named them Timandra, Phoebe and Philonoe. Each of their seven children had striking beautiful, blond hair, a rarity in Greece.

***

All Spartans had a tough life and only a very few of them were considered to be noble. Those that ruled as king were generally doing so in title only, and they were the leader in any of their military campaigns. Their wives were titled queen, but they weren't pandered to in the traditional sense. To be a king in Sparta was akin to being a ruling general. Unlike the other Greek States, Spartan kings reported to an elected council of Spartan freemen called "Ephors". The Kings they appointed were respected, admired, and often feared, but they could be replaced. Spartan Kings therefore needed to demonstrate competence and worthiness to remain in control.

Spartan women were all hard workers, be it in the house, or in the fields. They supported their husbands and encouraged male children into training to becoming accomplished warriors. Unlike other Greek girls, Spartan girls were also given responsibility, discipline, and education. They learned to become healers, midwives, meal preparers, and they managed serf farm workers and domestic slaves. Approximately one in four people in Sparta at the time of this story were slaves. Each family had one or two slaves and it was a normal part of Spartan life to have them do any or all of the menial tasks. They worked hard and for the most part, they were well treated.

All Spartan children were encouraged into athletic pursuits. They raced, played catch, and were awarded prizes to further encourage them to develop their skills. Spartans were like other Greeks in the way they made collective decisions. Many Greeks lived in towns, or villages, and the Greek word for them is "Polis." Free Greek men would meet in the towns to discuss policy, using politics and being political towards each other all for the common interests of the community and its inhabitants.

The Spartans however, resisted accepting the value of coins and preferred to barter. This reluctance alienated them from other city states who accepted coins from each other as a means of exchange. Spartan society was based on the practice that each Spartan was ready to assist other Spartans with whatever was needed. Very few of them would have been considered financially wealthy, as the accumulation of wealth was considered burdensome and unnecessary. They either made what they needed, or they simply took what they wanted from other nearby city states that were in conflict with them. Generally, they were frugal in their needs and wants. They placed little value on the arts and on culture. Only a few brief aspects about them was documented, as they preferred word of mouth communications, lessons, and storytelling.

All Spartan men were first and foremost fighting men. Each free Spartan citizen had first to be a skilled warrior, and then they had to have a trade. For example, they could be a warrior – blacksmith, or a warrior – craftsman, warrior – farmer. Each Spartan citizen had to complete military training and undertake trials and rituals and earn the right to fight with the other men. It was a tough life, but Spartan warriors were the most disciplined, respected, and feared of all the armies in their region.

Their classic military strategy was in having a protected flank, so that they could focus on fighting the enemy before them, knowing that the Spartan to the left and right of him, was protecting him from a side attack. They wore metal helmets, breast plates, and short tunics, that allowed manoeuvrability. They were armed with long thrusting spears that they never threw, and held massive shields which they used to pound into the enemy during close quarter combat. They had short, razor-sharp swords, which they used skilfully when their thrusting spear was no longer practical.

Their basic formation was a defensive block of warriors and they engaged the enemy as a team. Enemy armies fought battles based on them having superior numbers, with each soldier or warrior fighting as individuals. The Spartans didn't travel much. They had horses and despite being skilled in the saddle, they rarely risked using them in battle. Spartan warriors preferred the manoeuvrability of being on foot. The Spartan leaders generally fought defensively, and they had little interest in conquering neighbours.

Spartan warriors were often victorious against vastly superior numbers due to their continuous military training to improve their skills, teamwork, and disciplined mindsets. Their military strategies worked particularly well on flat ground.

Centuries later, the successes that the Roman legions achieved as a formidable army, had their foundations in Spartan disciplined military training and fighting strategies.

***

At about the same time, in a region named Calydon, Queen Althea wife of King OEneus gave birth to a son which they named Meleager. Althea was a doting mother and prayed to the gods for a fortunate life for their infant. Instead, to her consternation, she received a prophecy from the three Fates, Clotho, Lachesis and Atropos, that Meleager's destiny was such that when the wooden branch, just then burning in the fire was reduced to ash, that their son would immediately die. She quickly retrieved the branch and smothered it to extinguish the flames. The heat soon dissipated and she was able to secrete the timber away so as to preserve both it, and therefore her son's life.

***

Leda's and Tyndareus' children were given the most vigorous of Spartan training as each grew into adulthood. They became highly respected and trusted within Spartan society.  At sixteen years old both Castor and Polydeuces had passed their combat rituals and were accepted as junior warriors. Clytemnestra and Helen became of marrying age, with many men hoping that they would become the fortunate groom.

For a traditional Spartan wedding, the bride's hair was cropped short and her bridal clothing was from that of a boy. In this way it was deemed less of an entrapment as the groom hadn't been lured into marriage by his bride's beauty. After making a public vow that they be decreed to be husband and wife, the groom would perform a simulated act of coitus in public, to cement an everlasting relationship. After the festivities, he would return to live with the men and she'd return home to live with her parents. Later that night, he would secretly visit his new bride, pretend to capture her, take her to a discreet location where they'd copulate naturally. By the time a Spartan wife was ready to have children, her husband would have secured them a private home of their own. It would either be acquired through barter, or purposefully built for their personal and private use. Everyone helped and contributed, as promoting close family values was extremely important in Spartan culture.

Clytemnestra was persistently wooed by Agamemnon; King of Argos and it was with some reluctance that she eventually agreed to marry him. At their wedding, his brother Melelaus met her sister Helen, and he immediately desired for her to become his wife. Whilst he didn't impress her very much, he persisted, and so they too were eventually married. Both brides were still only sixteen years old on their wedding day, and their husbands were nearly twice their age. This was a common Greek custom with many believing that having an older husband ensured happiness, given that he would be experienced and therefore more mature and stable. Both families openly exchanged gifts to symbolise that the marriage was for mutual benefit and alliances were formally made. The girls left their family home and moved to live with their husbands. There were some visits made to see Leda and Tyndareus. Sadly, both girls were generally unhappy wives, but both were determined to remain loyal and faithful to their marriage vows.

Castor and Polydeuces were now twenty years of age. They continued with military training, ever prepared to take up arms to defend Sparta and to pursue Spartan interests. Both were excellent horsemen and Castor in particular, had a fondness for them, and so he learned how to "break in" the new horse's and prepare them for their riders.

Polydeuces grew to be heavier and had more bulging muscles than his slenderer, swifter, and more agile brother. Both were excellent boxers and wrestlers and loved to compete with each other, and with any others foolish enough to challenge them. They often teamed up, winning many fighting bouts and they became widely respected as young men of strength, speed, skill, and agility.

The other thing they had in common was their love for the daughters of Leucippus. The problem with this was the fact that Leucippus had already promised his daughters, Phoebe and Hilaeira, in marriage to their much older cousins, the twins, Lynceus and Idas of Messenia.

Castor and Polydeuces had previously experienced some unfortunate dealings with Lynceus and Idas. All four agreed and undertook a cattle raid in Arcadia. After stealing and securing the herd, they agreed to Idas' suggestion to an eating contest. The challenge was to see who could eat a steak meal the fastest. The winner got to divide the cattle into two herds. As they were all famished, they naively agreed. Idas then dared Castor and Polydeuces into eating bigger portions in order to prove their manliness. Again, because they were ravenous, and the wonderful smell of the roasting calf had captivated them, they again foolishly agreed. Idas and Lynceus quickly ate much smaller steaks and declared themselves the winners.

They then divided the cattle into smaller herds under the watchful eyes of Castor and Polydeuces. Idas then informed them that as he came first, he'd select the better of the two herds. Lynceus said as he came second, he'd settle for the second-best herd. Castor and Polydeuces were bewildered. They had been duped and went home without any of the stolen cattle. Now the thought of usurping these two thieves and cheaters really appealed to Castor and Polydeuces, as much as the prospect of sharing beds with Phoebe and Hilaeira.

'It is very fortunate brother, that it is a different sister that appeals to each of us.' Castor concluded.

'Yes, it is. I wouldn't like to fight you for mine,' Polydeuces winked with his reply.

'Because, you'd lose?' Castor asked mischievously.

'No, because you'd never forgive me for beating you,' he replied smiling.

They both laughed happily. They had admired Phoebe and Hilaeira from when they were young, and the twins often spoke about marrying them in a fabulous joint ceremony. Having learned that their love interests were betrothed to Lynceus and Idas didn't deter them at all, it just added lustre to the adventure. They were confident in the knowledge that both girls reciprocated their love, and their marriage plans for them, and were prepare to defy their father.

The brothers set off on horseback toward the village where Phoebe and Hilaeira lived with their parents. When they were within walking distance to the family home, they secured the horses to a tree and snuck into the village, and discreetly into their home.

Castor led Polydeuces through the darkened home, and into the girls sleeping chamber. They shook them awake and motioned them to be quiet. Both girls whispered in understanding, and they were clearly happy to see these suitors. Castor then indicated that they should follow them out and into the fields where they could talk. The sisters agreed, quickly dressed and then the four quietly returned to where the horses were tethered.

'It's safe for us to talk now,' Castor explained, and continued to speak in hushed tones.

'Talk!' Hilaria was astonished. 'I thought you were here to rescue us?' she teased.

'We are,' agreed Polydeuces. 'And we want to marry you.'

'Both of you?' Phoebe mocked.

'Well... only I want to marry you, Phoebe.' Polydeuces told her, 'Castor is in love with you, Hilaeira, and he really wants to marry you.'

Both girls then leapt into the arms of their blushing men. As they hugged, they planted kisses on them.

Castor was a romantic and only wanted to marry for true love. 'Are you happy because you truly want to be with us, or it is because we're rescuing you from them?'

'Castor. I love you. I know it isn't the Spartan way to marry for love, but that is what you'll have from me.' Hilaeira snuggled in closer into him and he was very happy.

There were some noises emanating from their father's house. 'I think we should leave now,' Polydeuces recommended.

'I see we each have a horse,' Phoebe observed and was impressed.

'We can travel faster with one rider per horse.' Castor remarked.

'You must have been confident that we'd be returning with you,' Phoebe laughed and planted another kiss on his cheek.

The four of them quickly mounted the horses and rode off toward the village that Castor and Polydeuces called home. When they arrived, they quickly explained their actions to Leda and Tyndareus, who were initially shocked at their son's behaviour. They were initially concerned about this causing massive disharmony between the two families. But, when they saw that the love and commitment that the four had had for each other, was so strong and determined, they capitulated and welcomed the girls into their family.

Despite some earlier threats from Leucippus, the girls' parents eventually accepted their daughter's decision. Soon both couples were married in a joint ceremony. The girl's parents attended the celebration and they happily conceded their daughters happiness.

Later Phoebe produced a son they named Mnesileos. Not long after that, Hilaeira gave birth to a son that they named Anogon. The two couples lived close by each other, were good friends, and for many years they lived and prospered, and all were happy and content.

***

Then one day, there was a visitor knocking on the door of Castor's family home. His name was Jason and he was on a quest. Long ago, he had learned about Castor and Polydeuces, and from their reputation had decided that he would invite them to join him.

Jason was a handsome young prince in his early twenties. He was from Thessaly, and was journeying across Greece to recruit brave men to join him in his adventure to secure the Golden Fleece. Jason needed the fleece to claim his birthright, the throne of Thessaly. The men who joined him in his quest would share in the spoils, the adventures, and camaraderie.

Jason had arrived by horse. He was dressed modestly so as to attract little interest in him as a traveller. His weapons, though readily accessible, were hidden amongst his clothing and saddlery. Whilst Jason was still youngish to be a leader, he was taller than most other men, and he was clearly strong from both exercise and hard labour. Jason was well versed, knowledgeable, exuded confidence, skilled with weaponry, and he therefore found it easy to earn respect.

'My name is Jason,' he said to the man who opened the door. 'I am seeking an audience with Castor and his brother Polydeuces. Can you tell me where I might find them?'

'An audience? Do you want them to perform for you?' Castor asked with a hint of a smile in his voice. 'Or, perhaps you're the entertainer and you want to enthral them with mirth and merriment.'

Jason wasn't easily dissuaded. He had journeyed for quite some time and had initiated this encounter with many men who had subsequently accepted his offer to join him in his quest. He replied carefully and with consideration in his choice of words. 'They may choose to perform for me. But first, I had better impress them with my reason for being here. I have a story to tell…'.

'A story teller! Are you any good?' Castor challenged.

Jason smiled. 'My story is still being written, but so far it has captivated the interest of many brave Greek warriors. I only want the opportunity to offer to share my adventure with both Castor and Polydeuces. They may want participate in what I'm sure will become an often-told Greek legend of endeavour and bravery.' Jason nodded affirming this introduction as an enticing challenge. It was his practiced technique use to intrigue the listener.

'I'll get my brother,' Castor capitulated. He was now interested and so closed the door to his own home, and motioned for Jason to follow him to another house.

'Thank you, Castor.' Jason smiled.

Castor stopped midway and turned to Jason.

'You already know me?'

'I do, but only from the way others have described you, and of course, by your well-earned reputation.' Jason was pleased that he had correctly guessed this man's identity. 'That is why I have sought both of you.' Jason added and placed a hand on Castor's shoulder as his symbol of trust and friendship. This was also a practiced technique.

Castor raised his hand and placed it on top of Jason's. He didn't push it away but squeezed it with some affection. Jason had already impressed him and the gesture was comforting. They broke and continued to walk toward Polydeuces' home.

Polydeuces answered the knock on his door. He examined the stranger that stood beside his brother. He then looked at Castor who nodded imperceptibly and Polydeuces immediately relaxed.

'I'll fetch wine,' Polydeuces concluded. Castor led Jason to some chairs that surrounded a long sturdy wooden table that was often used for larger outdoor gatherings. They sat and were soon joined by Polydeuces who had a jug of wine and three cups. He set them down and poured a generous measure of wine into each cup. The three men picked up the cups and saluted each other, drank, and then returned the cups to the table. The twins then made it clear that it was now up to Jason to explain why he had sought them out.

Jason started his story. 'I am a prince of Thessaly. My father, Aeson was usurped by my uncle when I was very young. For my protection, I was spirited away from Thessaly and was raised and tutored by Chiron.'

'The Centaur from Mount Pelion. We have heard much about him.' Polydeuces accepted this to be true. Castor nodded his agreement.

'Chiron taught me, and many others, about hunting and warfare. He was also particular about teaching music, poetry, the arts, and philosophy. I also now share some of his knowledge of medicine and healing. I am feel fortunate to have been his student,' Jason confirmed and then continued. 'When my studies drew to a close, I believed that I was ready to claim my throne. I returned home to the great city of Iolcus in Thessaly, and I was granted an audience by my Uncle Pelias, who is the unlawful ruler of my lands. When Pelias first saw me, he went pale. It was as if he had seen the spirit of his deceased brother. Apparently, the family resemblance between my father and I is very remarkable. He believed I had died during my birth, but my mother had tricked him into that belief, by having the midwives cry over my body as if I had not survived the delivery. My mother feared for my safety. As I was the rightful heir to my father's throne, my uncle would have been relegated to being regent and unable to complete his ambition to become the king. She feared for my life and so hid me, far away from my uncle.

Later, when we were alone, he reluctantly agreed that I did have a rightful claim to the throne. He acknowledged that he had deceived my father and had tricked him into granting him succession. He told me that he once intended to hold on to power until his death, but as he was getting old and feeble, and he now conceded that it would be soon time for him to step down.'

Jason drew a deep breath and continued. 'It turns out that his only son Acastus, has no interest in becoming king. Furthermore, Acastus respects my claim, so much so that he and I have become close friends, and he has also agreed to join me on my quest.' Jason smiled.

'Your quest is to reclaim your throne?' Castor sought clarification.

'It was once my only purpose, but my uncle is shrewd. He persuaded me into the belief that my taking the crown by force would destabilise the kingdom. He suggested that I should publicly earn my right to be their king, by performing a great feat. In this way I would secure my title by earning their respect, as opposed to achieving it with the use of force, or even using the threat of conflict. This thought process was consistent with my tuition that I had learned from Chiron, so I agreed for him to tell me more.'

'So, you are now on a quest to earn the respect of your people?' Polydeuces asked.

'What great feat must you perform? Castor added. He turned to his brother who nodded and they silently agreed that they were curious.

'In a faraway land, there is a Greek colony called Colchis. It is distance from here at the eastern edge of the known Greek civilisation, located on the eastern shore of the Black Sea,' Jason explained. 'Many years ago, my ancestors were involved in an escape from certain death by fleeing on the back of a giant winged ram that had a Golden Fleece. When they arrived, the ram was sacrificed to Zeus, and its fleece is now protected by a fierce dragon that never sleeps. My Uncle believes, and now so do I, that the Golden Fleece belongs to the people of Thessaly. I'm on a quest to go retrieve it from the dragon, and return it to our people.'

'How will that get you your throne?' Castor was dubious.

Jason smiled. 'Pelias has publicly committed himself to hand over the throne to me on my return with the fleece. He has formally put himself into a position to which he can no longer renege.'

'He also put you in the position, that if you don't complete the task, then you won't deserve your own throne,' Polydeuces added.

'That is true. I have had some time to consider this challenge. I've concluded that I could force the issue of my claim, but I'd risk having the people of Thessaly not supporting me. They have followed Pelias for a long time now, and many have prospered under his leadership. Or, I could follow this new path where I'll have earned their respect and admiration. Achieving this quest strengthens my claim and reduces the noble's resistance to my title.'

'The people do love a hero,' Polydeuces concluded.

'This is my opportunity to become one,' Jason agreed. 'I know I have the knowledge and skills required to be an effective ruler. The successes I achieve now with this quest will make my ascension more palatable for my subjects.'

'Colchis is a considerable journey. How will we get there?' Castor asked accepting Jason's need for agreeing to his quest.

'By ship,' Jason replied smiling.

Castor and Polydeuces burst into laughter. Jason was expecting it, as he had had the same reaction from others.

'My ship is very big,' he boasted smiling at them proudly. 'Enormous. It can comfortably carry fifty men with weapons and ample provisions.'

'No such ship ever existed,' Polydeuces scoffed.

'It does now,' Jason assured him. Jason produced a sketch drawing of the giant sea going vessel. Castor and Polydeuces studied the drawing with obvious amazement. Jason smiled as this part of the presentation was often the clincher. He then continued to explain, 'It is named the "Argo". My shipwright, Argus has built her using the finest timbers and workmanship.'

'Did he name the ship after himself?' Castor smirked.

'No. I named my ship the "Argo" in his honour. He has been loyal, resourceful, dedicated, inventive, an inspired leader of the construction team, and has accomplished a mighty service to us all. The Argo is a ship to be proud of.'

The twins nodded, indicating their respect.

Jason continued. 'Athena personally assisted us with her design, and she remained to guide us during construction. Even Hera has been benevolent to us with her support during assembly, by arranging a supply of sturdy oak timbers from her mother's grove at Dodona near Epirus.' Jason drew them nearer. 'Let me share something amazing with you… Our ships keel is divine oak and…' Jason hesitated.' '…the ship…she speaks to me.'

Jason's words hung in the air as the twins absorbed the significance of what they were hearing. Both Castor and Polydeuces murmured their respect for the achievement. Divine assistance added credibility to any adventure and Athena's assistance and Hera's approval and contribution of oak timbers from Rhea's sacred forests were therefore highly regarded.

'Fifty men. That is a lot of people. Who have you lured so far into your quest? Or are we the first?' Castor was intrigued.

'Many brave Greek warriors have accepted my invitation.' Jason beamed as he was now feeling confident that both brothers would join him in their support for his quest. 'Joining us will be Herakles, the great warrior and hero, son of Zeus. Also sailing with us is Meleager a prince from Calydon, Euphemus, Lynceus, Nauplius, Oileus, Talaus, Zetes and Calais. It is Tiphys that has had much experience with sailing in fishing boats, and so I've entrusted him with the helm.'

Both Castor and Polydeuces nodded approval.

'Theseus the famous hero who had killed the Minotaur, the Crommyonian Sow, and the Cretan Bull, is also joining us. And, Orpheus is sailing with us. He's no warrior, but I agreed to his joining our numbers, as he is well known as a prophet, musician, and poet, and at least one member of our crew should be able to sing our praises and tell the world our story of our adventures and ultimate glory.'

Both Castor and Polydeuces praised their support of his inclusion. The story of their endeavours, and how well it would be told, was also very important to them. Greek warriors loved a good action-adventure story, especially if they were featured admirably in it.

'Cepheus, the king of Tegea, Peleus, the king of the Myrmidions, and Laetes, the king of the Cephallenians also count themselves amongst us.' Jason was on a roll. 'Nestor is joining us as is Eurypylus, Idmon, Eurtion, Hippothous, Iphicles, Mopsus, and Telamon and his brother Peleus and many more.'

'What about Ancaeus?' Castor queried.

'Yes, Ancaeus is joining us, and he is bringing his legendary two headed axe.' Jason smiled. 'Oh, and Admetus, my cousin is defying his father's orders to join us also.'

'Could he be a spy?' Castor was concerned.

'I don't think so.' Jason hadn't considered this, and he now appeared troubled. 'He'd never have any opportunity to remit his observations. We'll be at sea.' He then shook his head. 'Besides, he's too pious to be untruthful.'

'See to it that he has no carrier birds amongst his possessions,' Polydeuces suggested.

The three men spoke long into the night. Both Phoebe and Hilaeira brought them food and refreshments. Later they attempted to persuade their husbands to talk more in the morning as it was late, and they should now come to bed to sleep. Unperturbed, Jason and his two newest Argonauts were engrossed in making detailed plans for the adventures to come.

The following morning, after a brief tearful farewell, the twins followed their Captain. They left behind their families after making promises of returning home having achieved great victories, increases in the families' wealth, and a significant boost to their reputations. Their wives and children obediently and resolutely watched them depart. Standing beside them was Leda and Tyndareus, who would watch out and care for them in their son's absence.

***

After an uneventful journey of many days, they reached the city of Iolcus, and the site of the Argo's berth at port. Jason was immediately confronted by his disgruntled crew. They were upset over a new arrival, a young woman named Atalanta. She had heard about Jason's quest, and had arrived to meet with him to volunteer to join his crew. She was reputedly skilled with bow and arrow, and with spears.

Atalanta could also run swiftly and everyone knew that she ran with Artemis as a fellow hunter.

She had a face that was too boyish for a girl, but too girlish to be a boy. But it was also widely reputed that her body was magnificent and her skin radiant, and for that reason numerous men had fantasised about being intimate with her. She was a source of lecherous discussion, though she did nothing to encourage it. Atalanta wore hunter's clothes with a vest that was held closed with a buckle of polished gold that hid her perfect female form well.

Meleager was immediately smitten by her. As he was yet to find a wife, he became increasingly determined to impress her with his own manliness, leadership, and hunting skills. Atalanta had noticed the interest that Meleager had shown toward her, but she did nothing to further excite his interest. She had long ago vowed her virginity, and had done much to make it plainly known of her disinterest in men as suitors, and openly discouraged their demands for sex.

In Jason's absence, a feud had developed between many of the men demanding that this be an all-male crew. Clearly, some were intimidated by her. He also learned that one man in particular, Meleager had fiercely stood up in full support for Atalanta's inclusion in the crew. The resentment over her presence was almost at boiling point by the time Jason had returned to the Argo with Castor and Polydeuces.

Immediately after the trio were welcomed, Meleager began to argue in favour of Atalanta's addition to the ship's company. Jason held up his hands to ask for calm. Behind closed doors he heard the individual reports of those that were the most vocal about Atalanta's participation as a member of their crew. After much deliberation and consideration, he marched to be in front of the crew, standing on a raised platform, he decisively made his pronouncement. 'The decision as to who should join the crew should be based on skills, their willingness and enthusiasm to make a contribution to the overall effort, and have a prevailing determination to be a part of this adventure. In my determination, Atalanta has all three.'

There were numerous "No's!" from many of the other men voicing objections.

Castor and Polydeuces were indifferent to her inclusion, but observed the exchanges between those that did with interest.

'Jason, please let her join us,' Meleager sounded desperate.

'Meleager, do you accept that this is my decision to make?' Jason challenged him and the few other men who were equally enthusiastic to have this attractive woman as part of the crew.

Meleager hesitated before replying. 'I do.'

Jason could see the effect Atalanta was having on this man, and he paused in thought. He then turned and spoke directly to the woman. 'Atalanta, would you meet with me privately to discuss your application?'

She nodded and followed Jason into his private meeting room. They sat and Jason poured wine and offered it to Atalanta. She accepted it and took a courtesy sip from the goblet. 'I know you only from your reputation,' he explained to her. 'I know you can match the skills of most of my crew.'

Atalanta said nothing.

'We'll be away at sea for a lengthy time and we'll encounter many unknown obstacles. I have no concern about your ability or courage to meet these challenges. My only real concern is the lust you'll engender from some of my men.' Jason let that hang in the air. He hoped it sounded like a compliment. In truth he felt it sounded like an admission that many men were weak when they were in the presence of a woman. 'Others will fear you, and some will fear for your safety and with that, they'll be compromised when coming to your aid.'

'That is true. I understand your concerns and I agree with them. I had hoped that these men would be more mature, and that they'd be able to accept me as an equal.' Atalanta looked solemn.

'The reality is that you are superior to many of my men and I believe they feel intimidated by you. I regret that this is the case, but I know in my heart that it is so...' Jason's voice trailed off.

'I'll withdraw,' Atalanta conceded.

'Thank you,' Jason said and he sounded relieved.

They stood up and Atalanta looked about the room looking for a discreet exit. Jason immediately understood and nodded. He showed her through some curtains that hid his private exit. After Atalanta had discreetly left the Argo's berth, Jason returned to his crew. He was relieved that no-one raised the subject, and that he did not have to explain Atalanta's absence.

***

The crew, under Jason's command, quickly provisioned the Argo and they were soon ready to make sail. A large group of well-wishers had gathered, which included some of the crews' wives and other family members. Some came to give encouragement, but others were hoping to dissuade individuals from departure.

The Argonauts and their Captain were all in high spirits and eager to set sail. The size and the magnificence of the Argo did attract the attention of the Nereids, a group of sea-goddess who marvelled at the Argo's size and stylish construction. They included Thetis, goddess of the spawning of marine life, Galene, the goddess of calm seas, and Psamathe, the goddess of sandy beaches. Their arrival was immediately taken as a positive omen as it was believed that their support would be of great benefit.

As Thetis approached the boat, she caught Peleus' attention. In a rare case of mutual love at first sight between a mortal man and a goddess, they talked extensively, laughed often, made love passionately, and before the Argo's departure, they were vowed to be wed. They agreed they would marry at Mount Olympus as soon as he had returned. Thetis promised that she'd watch out for him on his journey with Jason, and Peleus grinned with unrestrained happiness.

The Argonauts performed a short ceremony to acknowledge Athena's assistance with the construction of the Argo. They formally praised Hera for her support of the enterprise and then they made a traditional offering to Apollo, just to be sure. The talking beam cut from an oracular oak tree on Mount Pelion in Thessaly only spoke to Jason and shared its wisdom with him only when they were alone. 'It is time.' The beam advised him. Jason gave the commands and the ropes that held the Argo fast were untied. The Argo's sails caught the breeze and she turned and headed in a north-west direction following the Greek coastline. They intended securing additional fresh water, and provisions before eventually turning east and into the Aegean Sea.

For a while, both Castor and Polydeuces took turns in watching Admetus' behaviour. They observed that he was relaxed and his behaviour was normal and anticipated. They saw no method of communication with his father. They appraised Jason and all three agreed that Admetus was not a spy.

After many days sailing, the first place they visited was the island of Lemnos. The people of the island had a reputation of acting kindly toward sailors and visitors, and Jason hoped they'd quickly replenish the Argo with food and water, so that they could quickly depart. Jason didn't know that the islanders of Lemnos had just experienced a brief, but very disturbing event. For their support of Hephaestus during the worst of his troubled marriage with Aphrodite, the goddess punished the islands mortal inhabitants with a terrible curse. She condemned the women to excrete foul body odour. It was so bad that the men would not go near them. Despite washing and the application of pleasing body lotions, the noxious odour wouldn't dissipate.

The Lemnos men grew restless, and despite their urgent desire for female companionship and affection, they could not bear to be with their own women. Many men took their fishing boats and journeyed to Thrace, where they wooed and persuaded unmarried Thracian women to return with them to Lemnos to become wives and sweethearts. The woman of Lemnos did not take this development well. On the return of the men, with their new brides and concubines, they were set upon and brutally murdered by the angry spurned women. The Island of Lemnos became an Island of women. Over time, with Aphrodite's retribution now satisfied, the odour problem faded completely away. It was at this point that Jason and his crew of Argonauts arrived at the island. The reception they received was beyond any wildest imaginings.

Jason ordered the Argo be lashed to the crude stone jetty that served as a port for Lemnos. There was little activity with only a few women working in the fields of crops. The women stopped what they were doing, and watched the crew of the Argo disembark. One of the women whose name was Iphione, hoisted her skirts and ran to the township to share the news of the ship's arrival. The other women dropped tools and headed for the crew of the Argo. The Argonauts spilled onto the jetty and steadied themselves as they regained their land legs. The women that approached mingled with the men as if appraising them.

Jason tried to start a conversation with them. 'My name is Jason. My crew, the Argonauts and I, their Captain, require food and fresh water. We'll gladly pay for what you'll share with us, and we promise that we will not overstay our welcome.'

The women stared at Jason, saying nothing and were seemingly mute. There was no smiling or fearful reaction, no indication of understanding at all. One of the women began caressing the muscular arm of a crew member as if appraising him. Soon a large group of women came toward them. They marched briskly, but were without words or welcoming smiles. They were unarmed as far as Jason and his crew could tell. They abruptly stopped when they were close to the Argonauts.

'I am Jason, Captain of the Argo and these are my crew,' Jason told them.

'I am Hypsipyle, the Queen of Lemnos. You and your crew are welcome on our Island.' She then broke into a cheer and the women enthusiastically joined her by waving and cheering with great fervour. They then began to mingle with the crew. This had at first startled the Argonauts but as they were being swarmed by beautiful attentive women, so they quickly relaxed and began to enjoy the attention. Numerous conversations started and soon there was also laughter, as the women unabashedly flirted with the sailors.

Jason walked up to Hypsipyle. 'Where are the men of Lemnos?' he asked, trying to sound casual.

Everyone went suddenly still. No one moved. After a moment and with considerable calm, Hypsipyle replied. 'Sadly, all our males succumbed to a dreaded disease, and only we females survived. It has been many months since this occurred and we have grieved terribly for them. Polyxo, my advisor and mentor, believe that the danger has now passed and so there is no risk to you or your men. So, we're now happy to extend to you and your crew our generous hospitality.' She reached up and kissed him fully on the mouth. Other women took her lead and did the same to the men they fancied. Soon, as a group, they headed for the township. Forty-five of the men, including Jason, were now paired off with one or two women. Only Castor, Polydeuces, Herakles, Admetus, and Peleus remained with the ship, the women they spurned looked disapprovingly at them as they turned to follow the others.

'They are making a mistake,' Herakles scoffed and the others nodded in shared agreement, as they watched the departing village women walking arm in arm with their crew mates.

***

In the weeks that followed, the five remaining crew members kept busy with maintaining the ship. There was little for them to do, as the hull was still clean, the sails were still in good order, and the decks as yet, unspoiled. As the Argo was still on her maiden voyage, she was in excellent working order. Their food, drink, and other supplies were easily replenished, and the men had grown weary of playful banter. They were becoming bored.

On one occasion, both Castor and Polydeuces walked into the settlement to see what was happening. They received cheers from crew mates who mistakenly believed that they had come to join them in the revelry. As Castor and Polydeuces explored the settlement, they witnessed public fornication, drunkenness, and lethargy. Their shipmates were becoming degenerates. Their female hosts however, seemed alert, clean, and they were very watchful of the twins as they surveyed the deteriorating condition of their fellow Argonauts. They were unable to find Jason and were disappointed by the crews lack of knowledge of his whereabouts, and the women's lack of cooperation in assisting them in locating him.

Castor spoke to Meleager about what he had observed, but Meleager was drunk, and only sobbed about how much he missed Atalanta. Castor concluded by his two scantily clad female companions that he couldn't have missed her that much.

Next, they came across Orpheus. He was strumming his Lyre and singing his latest composition. He was evidently affected by the wine as his voice was audibly off key, and well below his usual standard and pace. His new song was another lament about the tragic loss of his deceased wife, and the betrayal he now felt by allowing himself to enjoy female companionship and their blatant affections. He had no idea where Jason, or any of the other men were, but he promised to explain to them that they should return to the Argo when he saw them. Both Castor and Polydeuces shook their heads in dismay. Resigned, the twins withdrew and returned to the ship to report the crew's disposition.

Castor, Polydeuces, Herakles, Admetus, and Peleus next had a group meeting to decide what they should do.

'Clearly we shouldn't allow this behaviour to continue for much longer,' Castor suggested.

'I'm here for adventure and a sea voyage,' Herakles agreed.

'I thought you needed a rest from adventure,' Admetus challenged.

'My close friend Chiron was accidently wounded by my own poisoned arrow. The king thought I could do with a sea change before resuming my eleven tasks,' Herakles explained.

'I thought you had to perform ten tasks.' Polydeuces queried.

Herakles sighed. It seemed everyone knew all about his life's story. 'It was supposed to be ten, but the killing of the Hydra at lake Lerna was disallowed, as the king claimed I had too much assistance from my nephew.'

'Iolaus.'

'Yes.'

'Wasn't Athena also helping you?'

'She was more of a witness to the event,' Herakles explained for the umpteenth time. He drew a deep breath. 'I graciously accepted the king's determination, so I still have seven more tasks to complete for him. If we don't resume this quest for the Golden Fleece soon, I may decide to abandon you all here, and return to the mainland to continue doing them.'

'I wonder what messy job you'll have to do next,'

They were silent for a while whilst they pondered Herakles next challenge.

Eventually, Castor spoke and made a suggestion to the others. 'I think we should do some training.'

They all nodded their agreement.

'Um, I'm not skilled with either sword, or bow and arrow,' Admetus admitted.

'Perhaps, this would be the opportune time to remedy that deficiency,' Herakles observed.

'Oh, I thought, I might be excused.'

'Nonsense, being skilled with weaponry might save your life one day.'

So, for the next few weeks the five men, ran, practiced with wooden swords, and threw spears. Soon, even Admetus was achieving competency and confidence.

Peleus was delighted when Thetis paid them a surprise visit. She had been monitoring their progress and was concerned when the Argo had remained at Lemnos for such a long time. The five men explained the condition of their fellow crew mates, and how the weak minded had allowed themselves to be to be lured away by the promise of debauchery.

She spent her nights with Peleus and her days watching the men train. She didn't mention the whereabouts of Galene or Psamathe, her fellow goddesses of the seas, but the men agreed that they must be close by.

'How are you at boxing, Castor?' Herakles challenged.

'Polydeuces is the man you should challenge. He is the boxer in the family.'

'Polydeuces?'

'Certainly,' he rose to his full height as he accepted the challenge.

The two men stripped off their shirts and took position on a grassy area adjacent the ship. They wrapped their fists with cloth and Castor assisted them both as these bindings would protect their own knuckles, and their opponents face and torso, by dampening the blows to come.

Naturally, Castor wanted his brother to win, but he refrained from saying anything. The others took station on the deck, and Castor joined them when he had finished assisting with the preparations. From the ship they had a better view, plus they were less likely to be in the way of unintended blows as the fight progressed.

As an audience, they were quite subdued. Everyone was curious as who would be proven to be the superior fighter. If they had a favourite, all were reserved enough to keep it to themselves.

At first, both Herakles and Polydeuces tested each other, throwing out jabs as they moved in a boxer's dance, favouring a defensive posture, each taunting the other. Suddenly, Herakles landed a solid left hook. Polydeuces absorbed the blow and retaliated with a quick succession of a combination of punches to the ribs and abdomen that pushed Herakles backward.

Herakles took the blows and seemed to be bidding his time, waiting for an opening. When the opportunity presented itself, he performed a mighty uppercut that shook and rattled Polydeuces.

Both men persisted with raining blows on the other and Polydeuces lip was split, but they continued punching as the intensity of their fight grew. The watchers understood that this had become a battle of wills, where neither man was willing to concede defeat, no matter how tired or hurt they were. Herakles landed another vicious blow to the body, but the undaunted Polydeuces countered with a vicious cross. There was a flurry of punches when Herakles made his move, but Polydeuces dodged a haymaker and Herakles lost his balance. Polydeuces landed a blow on Herakles back, and he dropped to the grass. Herakles swiftly pivoted to defend with his feet, but Polydeuces was waiting for Herakles to regain his stance and resume the fight. Both men were exhausted and were sweating profusely. More half-hearted punches were thrown, but all missed their opponent. Slowly, in a boxers embrace, they collapsed to the ground leaving both men gasping desperately for deep lungsful of air. Bruises began to show and it was evident that both would be in prolonged pain as they recovered.

Neither man spoke, neither man claimed victory, neither man conceded defeat.

The others disembarked the ship and gathered around the two brave boxers. They began to administer aid, helping them to bind their damaged torsos and pounded appendages, that were now swollen from the fierce blows. Their hands were also swollen, and they were both in a weakened position.

As Herakles regained his voice, he asked the spectators. 'Who won?'

'I believe this is the type of fight that you would declare it a draw.' Castor explained.

'I'm okay with that,' Polydeuces agreed.

'One of us must have been better than the other, surely?' Herakles wanted a victory.

'You are both skilled and exceptional fighters,' Peleus proclaimed. Thetis nodded her agreement. She abhorred violence.

'Admetus?'

'I don't have enough boxing knowledge to be able to make that determination. I have on occasion, witnessed other men box, and in my unqualified opinion, your mastery and use of your boxing expertise were far superior to those that I've seen before. I also note the modest nature of the injuries that you have sustained. I can only conclude that if this was a real fight, where your life was in actual danger, that you may have been somewhat more strategic and perhaps less conservative and unrestrained. I do not box, and I will do all I can to avoid it. I'm not even sure that I'll be of much use to my side in an actual battle, despite my improved ability with sword, spear, and archery. I'm sorry, but I must agree with the others that you were evenly matched.'

***

Jason and his crew had made the most of the warm and passionate welcome that they received. They had indulged in the islands supplies of food and drank the wine that obviously needed drinking. They enjoyed the sex, the massages, the food, and other sensual pleasures that the women were more than eager to share with them. Many babies were conceived during their stay on the Island of Lemnos. Some of the men were beginning to want to form permanent attachments to the women they bedded, but all were politely reminded by these women, that they were only temporary guests, and that they should just relax and enjoy themselves.

Even Jason was considering abandoning his quest, and he spoke about his internal conflict with Hypsipyle, whilst they lay naked in her bed, spent from exhaustive copulation. 'I have developed a great fondness for you, Hypsipyle,' he explained to her, as if their many nights of exclusive lovemaking hadn't already demonstrated this fact.

'I feel the same way about you,' she conceded.

'If you like, I could abandon my quest for the Golden Fleece and stay here with you,' Jason suggested with a degree of sincerity.

'You would grow to hate me, if you did that,' she countered.

'Perhaps, I could complete my quest, and then return here to you,' he proposed looking bright eyed with expectation.

'When you have the fleece, you'd return to your own people as their champion. You'll fulfill your destiny and become their king, and you'd soon forget me,' she told it how she understood it.

'I wouldn't!' Jason was hurt.

'But you must complete your quest. You and your men need to do this, or as you grow old, you'll come to regard yourselves as failures. You must go, and even though you'll encounter many impediments and obstacles, you must prevail. Some of you, possibly even you, Jason, will die in your attempt, but it must be done.' She seemed genuinely sincere to Jason and he listened to her words with respect.

Hypsipyle continued. 'You may even find true love with another woman. It is best that you do not think of me, or plan to return to me or my bed. Focus only on your goals.'

'I'd never...' he started to contradict her.

She kissed him fully on the mouth to dissuade him from speaking further. She broke away and continued explaining. 'You may be gone for so long that when you do return, I'll be old and unattractive.'

Jason looked defeated.

***

The following morning Jason headed for the Argo. It had been a while since he'd checked up on his ship, or the crew that remained with her. He was pleased to see that she had been kept in good order by the five men who had volunteered to remain with the ship.

'Herakles!' Jason greeted him with a wave as he approached the Argo.

'Come up to the deck, Jason is here!' Herakles called down to the others. Individually, Castor, Polydeuces, Admetus, and then Peleus came on deck and they descended the boarding ramp to greet their Captain. Jason stood before them and marvelled at their finely perfected physiques. They seemed to have developed muscles on their muscles. His men laughed as Jason stared.

'We've been working out!' Castor explained.

'We have been running, throwing, wrestling, and exercising with our swords and spears. Even Admetus has trained, and he has much improved with the use of bow and arrows,' Herakles declared.

'Herakles and I are evenly matched in boxing,' Polydeuces proudly announced as Herakles winced but grinned.

Jason examined himself. His arms and waist were showing advanced signs of flabbiness. 'I have been away for too long,' he concluded.

'It was only twelve weeks,' Peleus informed his Captain.

Jason was in shock. He hadn't realised they had been at Lemnos for amount of time. The food, wine, and indulgent intimacy, had inflicted a detrimental effect on Jason's body. He now felt weak compared to these healthy strong men.

'You should gather the crew. You should all immediately commence training, and as soon as you are all strong and fit again, we should resume our voyage,' Herakles advised.

'I agree.' Jason replied solemnly. He privately chastised himself for allowing this deterioration to happen.

The five men cheered as this was the news that they'd been waiting for. They were smiling and happy that their captain had finally come back to them.

***

When Jason returned to the village, he found Hypsipyle, and painstakingly informed her of his decision to depart with his crew. Despite her earlier advice, he was still a bit disappointed when she wasn't saddened about his decision to leave Lemnos.

Hypsipyle caressed his face. 'We will assist you with provisioning your ship with water and food for the next leg of your journey. When will you depart?'

'In seven days.'

'Your men should return to your ship now. Separation will be difficult for some of them.' Hypsipyle was acknowledging that there could be issues.

'My men will obey my orders,' Jason assured, hoping this would be true.

Jason and Hypsipyle exited her home and she issued instructions to messengers. Soon everyone knew that the Argo and her crew would be leaving the island in seven days' time.

As Jason found his crew, his announcement produced many saddened faces. But to Jason's surprise, there were no significant objections. Jason and his crew said their tearful goodbyes to their female companions. Some men made promises to return in the future. On the same day of Jasons decision, they returned to the Argo in small groups. Soon, they all were assembled and accounted for.

For the next seven days, the Argonauts camped near their ship. They ate healthy foods, drank only water, trained with weapons, and exercised vigorously. In between their training they stowed on board the promised supplies that were delivered by the women. There were no tearful demonstrations during these consignments. The women simply delivered the supplies of water and food to the boat, and then quickly returned to their township.

Early on the morning of the seventh day, the Argo and her crew departed. They set sail with the wind in an easterly heading, and were journeying toward the sunrise. The women of Lemnos were nowhere to be seen.

***

For several days, the gentle wind Zephyrus moved the ship closer to their next adventure. Soon the Argo passed by Hellespont and entered the Sea of Marmara. They eventually arrived at the island of Propontis, which was also known as Bear Mountain, so named as its silhouette was shaped like a resting bear. The people of Propontis were famed for mining the high-quality white marble, and its export revenue provided the inhabitants much welcomed income. Some of its inhabitants, the Doliones, who proudly claimed to be descendants of Poseidon, were gathered in the merchant port to welcome them.

As the Argo crew secured the ship to the dock, they were met with cheers as they were warmly greeted by King Cyzicus and his followers. 'We welcome Jason and his Argonauts to our island home.' Within the assembled crowd, was a large group of attractive women and they too applauded their approval. King Cyzicus was now holding up his arms to get everyone's attention. 'In celebration of your amazing quest, we have arranged a banquet in your honour.' The crowd cheered once more and this time the crew of the Argo joined in, delighted at the prospect of a cooked meal, some wine, and the possibility of the evening ending with desirable companionship in a soft bed.

Jason descended the ramp and was affectionately embraced by the king. He and his crew then followed the king and his retinue, and his other loyal subjects into the town where they lived. In the market place, tables and chairs had been arranged in preparation of their arrival. Food trays brimming with cooked meats, vegetables, and fruits, and numerous jugs of wine were being arranged on the massive serving tables. Musicians were preparing to entertain the multitude. The crew relaxed and were delighted with the warm reception the people of Propontis had prepared for them. Everyone was friendly and happy. The feast soon turned into a party and the wine was having its effect. Jason and Cyzicus were seated next to each other at the head table. In a playful banter, they were toasting each other's greatness, each trying to outdo the other.

During a moment of clarity, Jason requested to his host. 'We'll require some fresh water and provisions for the ship.'

'We only have limited water supplies and limited food.' Cyzicus replied apologetically. 'Your visit to us came as a surprise, and we have used much of our reserves in your honour for this feast.' He explained smiling.

Jason was confused. 'But you seemed to be expecting us?'

'In a manner,' Cyzicus laboured to explain. 'Other sailors sighted your ship docked at Lemnos as they sailed past. Then recently, a fisherman spotted you on the horizon. We even had some lookouts posted high up the mountain, so we knew to expect you. Your quest is big news, and so we wanted to be ready for your arrival.' He paused. 'Actually, we had thought it would be much sooner…?'

Jason reflected on the pleasures they had received by the women of Lemnos. 'The length of our stay was unanticipated.'

'I bet it was.' Cyzicus laughed and slapped Jason on the arm jovially. Then he became serious. 'We will share with you what we can.'

Jason felt guilty. 'Can we repay you in some way?' he proposed, hoping his offer wasn't deemed offensive toward his host and his generosity.

Cyzicus shook his head and smiled. 'We are proud to be a small part of your quest. All I ask is that you remember us well with the numerous retellings of your story.'

'That my friend, we will proudly do,' Jason confirmed. He really liked this king and his people, and he was pleased that they had decided to visit here.

Cyzicus then offered the solution to their provision requirements. 'There are some fresh water springs only a three-day trek from here. There you can refill your water barrels.  Also, you may hunt some of the wild animals that live in that area,' he added, nodded in an affirming manner, before adding. 'But please, only take what you really need, as we all need to hunt for food also.' Cyzicus then winked and grinned benevolently.

Jason slowly nodded his acceptance and understanding. He had seen livestock on their way from the port to the town. The feast they had eaten was from farmed and recently butchered animals. There must be a reliable water source to be able to achieve this. These people didn't need to hunt to eat.

Cyzicus was about to add that they shouldn't venture to the south side of the island, but both men became distracted by Herakles showing off with a display of strength. He held two women in each arm high above the ground. They shrieked with a combination of fear and excitement, and the revellers laughed and applauded as they were enjoying the spectacle.

By now Orpheus was also in full form. He was strumming his Lyre and singing a popular bawdy ballad and his crew were enthusiastically joining in, as were many of the locals. There was much laughter and shrieking as inhibitions continued to relax. Jason inwardly winced and hoped that this night wouldn't denigrate into a still, all too familiar, Lemnos experience.

***

The following day, the Argonauts divided into three teams. The first team stayed with the ship. The second team set off to refill water barrels. Admetus was in the third team and was proud to demonstrate his improved skills with bow and arrow, and he accounted for three of the eight beasts that they hunted and killed. The men butchered and preserved the meat in salt barrels. The two away teams returned to the Argo and the crew stowed the provisions.

Later that day, King Cyzicus invited Jason and some of his crew to journey with him to the summit of Bear Mountain. He assured them the assent was worth the effort as the view from the top was magnificent. Many agreed to undertake the climb, but when they reached the summit and to their dismay, they could see that the Argo and her remaining crew were under attack. A renegade band of twelve-foot-high giants, known as the Gegenees, each with six arms, were now hurling stones and spears at the Argo and her defending Argonauts. Herakles, Castor, and Polydeuces were on board, and they were able to hold them off, with their own arrows and spears that they accurately propelled into the assailants, killing several of them.

The climbers now hastily descended the mountain to join in the Argo's defence. The remaining fleeing giants were set upon by Jason and his crew, and by King Cyzicus and his soldiers, and they were quickly defeated. King Cyzicus was sincerely apologetic, as he had forgotten to warn Jason and his crew about these giants. Jason suspected that the climb up the mountain was a lure that Cyzicus used to draw out these giants, and that he had hoped that the Argonauts would rid him of an ongoing problem. None of his men were hurt or killed during the encounter, so he relaxed and decided to dismiss these suspicions.

***

The following morning, Jason and the crew of the Argo set sail once more. After several hours of sailing, they rounded the eastern tip of the island when a fierce storm surprised them by descending on the Argo. Its strong head winds, huge waves, and heavy rain, pounded the ship and so they decided to return to bear island to seek shelter in a protected bay on the islands southern shore, and wait out the worst of the storm. Jason sent some of his men off the ship to tether it to several points on shore to prevent the Argo being swept away or dashed against the rocks.

To his dismay, his men were immediately set upon and slaughtered by heavily armed soldiers that were guarding the bay. The crew didn't wait for orders. Even though the surf was fierce, the Argonauts dove off the Argo, weapons in hand, to race up to the beach to avenge their comrades. The battle was brief but deadly, with many of the soldiers who were guarding the bay now lying deceased, as were several of their fellow crew mates. Jason was distressed when he recognised that one of the men, that he himself had killed, was his new friend, Cyzicus.

Later, when a truce was finally established, Jason learned from one of Cyzicus' adult sons, that this bay was frequented by pirates who often raided the nearby inhabitants under cover of a storm. They had established a permanent guard who were posted to thwart these pirates. They had established an effective communication system that allowed the king and his guardsmen to quickly respond with required support for these guards. Now Cyzicus lay dead at Jason's feet. His crew were despondent at the unnecessary loss of life, and so they arranged and performed an elaborate funeral service to honour the deceased, so that all of them could mourn their dead properly and with dignity.

'This is a miserable day, brother,' Castor spoke in mournful tones.

'Yes, it is,' Polydeuces agreed. Both had lost friends. They had lost friends before, but doing so in this way, made it feel worse.

Before setting sail once more, the Argonauts cut their hair short as a mark of remorse and grief at what had happened.

***

The Argo sailed for many days and soon the men were in need of fresh water supplies. As they sailed neared the jagged coast of Mysia, Herakles snapped his oar on submerged rocks. The other men teased him and all were ordered to raise oars by Jason when he confirmed that there was further risk. When they found a safe point to anchor, Herakles set off to find a fallen tree that was suitable to make a replacement for his oar. The others went off to look for water to replenish their barrels and for prey to hunt. When the provisions were stowed, Herakles had still failed to return with his replacement oar. Eurtion suggested that he'd go off in search of Herakles and Jason allowed it. Before he left, he was urged to return by dawn the following day, or they'd set sail without them.

Jason had intended the warning to be only a joke, but two of his other crew took the opportunity to make mischief. Zetes and Calais were jealous of Herakles' reputation and commanding position within the crew. When Herakles and Eurtion failed to return the following day, they urged Jason to make good on his promise to abandon their crew mates and make sail without them.

Castor, Polydeuces, and Telamon urged that they should wait, and Jason readily agreed and delayed their departure. Later that day, he was visited by Glaucus, a mortal who had turned into an immortal God of the Sea after eating the local herbs. Glaucus explained to Jason that Herakles and Eurtion were safe and that they were now on board a vessel that was bound for Greece. Herakles had apparently agreed to return home when encouraged by Glaucus to complete his labours and to finally rid himself of Hera's curse. It was thus that Jason reluctantly decided to make sail and leave without two of his crew. He never learned that Glaucus had been only been told of Herakles departure by Zetes and Calais, and that his information was only hearsay.

When Herakles and Eurtion returned to the shore carrying his new oar, they discovered to their dismay that the Argo had sailed without them.

***

Many days later they sighted a town and Jason decided they should approach, drop anchor and ask for provisions. From the ship Jason called to the townspeople. 'My name is Jason and my ship the Argo and my crew wish to trade for food and fresh water.'

'You and your crew are welcome at Bebryces.' A man wearing fashionable headdress replied.

They dropped a small dingy and Jason, Castor and Polydeuces rowed to the shore to meet with the onlookers.

'I am Amycus, king of the Bebryces,' the man with the headdress introduced himself.

'I'm Jason, and these are two of my crew, Castor and Polydeuces,' Jason completed the introductions.

'We are delighted to host you and provide for you.' Amycus told them smiling. 'You'll pay us his weight in gold,' he said pointing to Polydeuces. 'And we'll let you leave with as much food and water as you can carry.'

Jason, Castor, and Polydeuces initially laughed, but were soon puzzled when neither the king nor his entourage joined in the merriment. Clearly to them, this wasn't a joke.

'Regretfully, that amount exceeds our purse,' Jason bowed his remorse.

'Then you, your ship, and your men, are ours to keep, and you'll work for us to earn your food and shelter as our permanent guests,' King Amycus informed them. This time he and his townspeople did laugh as they really enjoyed this part of welcoming new arrivals.

The three men reached for their swords and were about to flee, when spears suddenly materialised and were accurately aimed at their bellies. They reluctantly sheathed their swords and tried to look humble. Many boats had now surrounded the Argo and the crew were quickly overwhelmed by the sheer number of boarders. Jason signalled to his crew that they should offer no resistance.

'Would you perhaps have a third option?' Jason asked hopefully. He was trying to stall them for some time, in order to think of a way out of this mess that suddenly had escalated.

Amycus and his people roared into laughter. After they settled, he sighed and smiled. 'Yes, there is, my forlorn friend. But I think you won't accept it,' he challenged.

'What is it?' Jason asked hoping he'd not regret the answer.

'I like to box,' Amycus explained. 'My people will no longer indulge me, as they have seen too many depart this world on route for Hades.'

'I've had some boxing experience,' Polydeuces offered.

Amycus examined Polydeuces more closely. 'You do have the physique, but do you have the strength, skill, and the endurance? You can see that I'm truly formidable,' he explained as he laughed once more, evidently entertained by the Argonauts predicament.

'If I should win and you acknowledge me as the victor, will you re-provision us from your own purse and allow us to continue our journey?' Polydeuces asked cautiously.

'I think the odds favour me!' Amycus laughed once again.

'Declare it, and I will fight you,' Polydeuces invited so that the deal could be struck.

'I, King of the Bebryces, do declare that should this man...'

'Polydeuces.'

'... Polydeuces, defeat me in a boxing match, that we will fully provision them at my expense, and that we will allow all of them to continue with their journey.'

The crowd cheered enthusiastically, relieved to be entertained by a boxing match that didn't include one of their own people.

Amycus removed his headdress and passed it to an assistant. He then dropped his clothing, Polydeuces followed suit. The fists flew for many minutes with both men managing to avoid the others reach. The crowd cheered each time the king threw his punch, and this energised Amycus. Soon, he grew more desperate to make his mark on Polydeuces, and carelessly swung out a wide punch that left him unguarded. Polydeuces seized the opportunity and struck the left side of Amycus' face with a lightning-fast blow. Amycus fell heavily to the ground. His assistant examined him and slowly shook his head. Amycus was dead.

Polydeuces stood still, naked to the world, and awaited the crowd's reaction. Some of the men with the spears immediately attacked and Castor threw Polydeuces sword to him. The battle was swift and decisive, as Amycus's soldiers were quickly defeated. Jason looked to his crew who were all standing with the boarders watching the skirmish on land. There wasn't a fight on the ship. To Jason and his crews surprise, the remaining soldiers and townspeople now cheered and applauded the victor's. They had just defeated their tyrant king and his cronies, and had liberated the good people of Bebryces.

Both Jason and Castor sighed deeply in relief. Jason signalled the crew on-board the Argo that all was well. They had watched from the ship and were glad that Polydeuces had won but were also concerned with the ramifications of his victory. Relieved that the townspeople were now celebrating, they too could relax. The Bebrycrian's quickly voted for a new popular leader, and they were invited to celebrate at a feast that continued well into the night. The following morning, they were given some live sheep, other food including cakes and biscuits, and ample fresh water to be able to continue their quest.

***

The Argo continued to sail farther east and soon came close to Salmydessus. Both Zetes and Calais begged Jason to drop anchor so that they could visit their sister Idaea, wife of Phineus the local King. Jason was hesitant given their recent experiences with the Bebrycrian's. Zetes and Calais pressed their request by explaining that Phineus had the gift of prophecy and might be useful with information valuable to Jason in obtaining the Golden Fleece. Jason reluctantly consented, and the Argo dropped anchor. Soon Jason, Zetes and Calais set off in the small boat to find Idaea and her husband Phineus.

As they approached the building, they noticed that it appeared neglected and deserted. They became instantly cautious, fearing the worst. The three men ascended the steps and entered what appeared to be the main room of the palace. There they found Phineus alone, starving, blind, and so weak that he could hardly move.

Zetes rushed to his brother-in-law and held his hand. 'Phineus, it is I, Zetes.'

The old man managed a smile. He recognised the voice and was glad to hear it. 'Zetes.' He crocked and coughed into his hand and then reached out with his other hand in an attempt to embrace his brother-in-law.

'I'm with here with Calais and my captain, Jason of the Argo.'

'Calais, you are here also?' He smiled beckoning the other man to come closer.' Calais did as bid and the three embraced.

'Our sister...?' Calais asked after her.

Phineus looked crest fallen. 'I do not know.' He paused and looked about though blind. 'She may be dead. We've had a challenging and difficult time.'

'Tell us Phineus, tell us what has happened here,' Zetes asked the old man, desperate to understand and to make a difference.

Phineus cleared his throat. 'For a long time, we were all happy and content. Life was good and we had many visitors, they brought gifts and food and wine with them, all for an opportunity to meet with me.

We'd hold hands and I'd look deeply into their eyes, even though I already knew what I was going to say.' He smiled. 'I had learned early to add mystique to my accounting of my paying visitor's future lives...'

'So, you shared your gift in exchange for reward,' Calais spoke his thoughts aloud to no one in particular.

'These visitors took up much of our time, crops were neglected, the buildings couldn't be maintained, and our farm animals disappeared all the time. I had to demand ever increasing payment for my prophecies. Many of them came true you know, but that just added to my fame and demand from the number of people who wanted to meet with me continued unabated.' Phineus paused remembering the chaotic days of being a commercially successful seer.

'Then one day a messenger came from Zeus. I was going to be punished for revealing too much about the future to human mortals. He claimed I was altering the balance of power, and that Zeus was now angry with me. I explained that I simply wanted to help people. I was frightened and pleaded for mercy, promising that I would desist from sharing my visions, but the messenger told me that it was too late. I suddenly knew my fate, one that I should have foreseen.' He looked puzzled. 'Then the Harpies arrived... do you know about them?'

'They are the sudden gusts of wind that can do much damage,' Jason offered.

'Yes, yes, they are sudden, and they can be powerful. They can blow a ship off course you know? At first my visitors stopped coming. I learned later that it was the Harpies that had blown those boats away from my shore. Some enterprising visitors landed farther west from here and came to me on foot, but the Harpies quickly learned of this, and tormented them with such strong gusts that forcibly turned them around. Quickly, word spread of my punishment and they were now abandoning all endeavours to see me. As my supply of food and gifts stopped coming, we ran out of food and we were hungry and so had to fend for ourselves. My wife, your sister, and all of my people left to find food, supplies…, but they never returned. I fear for them.'

'Next, the Harpies blew inside my palace, it is now quite a mess as you can see. Did you know that they are able to transform into hideous bird like women, and that they pecked viciously at me, and they shit all over the place?' The Argonauts looked about the room at the mess and nodded. Phineus continued explaining, 'They howled and shrieked and stole my food, and thieved all my possessions. Podarge is the worst of them. That ugly witch inflicted this.' He pulled up the dirty sleeve of his robe to reveal an old festering gash on his arm.

'How long ago did this happen? How long did it go on for?' Jason asked looking about for recent signs of an attack. He noticed that there were many feathers scattered amongst the debris of Phineus' household.

'They come daily,' Phineus replied with a heavy sigh. 'Each afternoon they come in from the north.'

Jason turned to Zetes and Calais. 'We must do what we can to stop this from happening.'

'How?' Zetes and Calais asked together.

Phineus cleared his throat and made a suggestion. 'Perhaps, you could appeal to Cleopatra, she might be able to help. So far, my appeals to her have gone unanswered.'

'Cleopatra? Your first wife?' Zetes queried. 'How can she…?'

'She is the daughter of Boreas; god of the north wind and she may agree to ask him on my behalf to rid me of these Harpies,' Phineus explained.

'Jason, can we do this?' Zetes appealed for the sake of his brother-in-law.

'I'll try to figure out what we can do,' Jason replied. 'You stay here and feed Phineus. Clean him up and for pities sake, attend to that wound,' he ordered and then paused, thinking. 'I'll return to the Argo and see if I can organise the men to prepare some kind of traps to capture these Harpies.'

Jason returned alone to the Argo and organised his men with nets and ropes that they would need to capture, and then hopefully banish the Harpies. They would need to accomplish this feat whilst they were in their monster form. He accepted that when they were in their wind form, they would have no chance of succeeding. He decided they'd position themselves in strategic points within the building in groups of four men, with each team ready to overwhelm and capture an individual Harpie.

Jason next consulted the oracular oak that advised him. He asked the godlike timbers about their chances of succeeding.

'You will capture them, and I'll summon Boreas and demand that he blows these Harpies away forever,' the talking ancient timber beam assured Jason.

The brave fighting men of the Argo had positioned themselves in their designated hiding places, armed with shields, nets, and spears. The evil winds arrived and they were already starting to pick up speed. As the Harpies had caught the scent of fresh food in Phineus' possession, they materialised in order to snatch it away from him.

They shrieked and howled, and flew about the palace buffeting Phineus, Zetes, and Calais, and were pelting them with debris.

Then Boreas appeared and his wind was stronger than the combined force of the Harpies frightening them into panicked confusion. The Harpies retreated in terror, straight into the traps prepared by Jason and his men. They were quickly imprisoned, and as the men were about to plunge their swords and spears into the bird-women, Iris, goddess of the rainbow appeared through the opening and entered the palace. 'Stop!' Iris commanded and all obeyed. The pointy ends of their weapons poised. Everyone froze in inaction, man and Harpie alike, such was her power.

Iris was well known as a messenger of both Hera and Zeus. Her luminescence projected her many radiating colours in the room dazzling the men. In awe of her, they lowered their weapons. Iris then materialised in human form and surveyed the scene. 'I'm here under direct orders from Zeus. He will grant Phineus a reprieve from the Harpies torment, if you agree to release them unharmed.'

Jason looked around him assessing the situation. He then physically relaxed. 'We agree,' he confirmed. He then motioned his men to free the Harpies which they did, and with a final shriek they transformed into wind and blew away forever. Boreas next materialised, bowed his head, smiled, and then he too disappeared.

'Zeus asks that you refrain from making so many prophecies. He cannot abide it,' Iris explained the compromise to Phineus. 'You must restrain yourself.'

'I agree,' Phineus nodded and smiled.

Iris faded away and the sun shone brilliantly on Phineus's palace. Jason and his crew spent some time with the king. Over the next few days, the Argonauts did much of the cleaning and tidying of the palace and did repair work on the buildings. They also nursed Phineus and the effect of regular meals and clean clothes was remarkable. His sight was slowly returning and his health and strength was improving daily.

Soon, the townspeople were happily returning and they quietly and obediently were resuming their duties, as they were no longer fearful of the Harpies. Regrettably, there was no news of what became of Idaea. Phineus, Zetas and Calais were now resolved that they'd never learn of her fate.

When Jason felt it was time to leave Phineus and resume their journey, they replenished the Argo's stores, and prepared to depart. As the crew reboarded, Phineus drew Jason aside. 'Goodbye my friend. Your deeds here will be praised for eternity. I've now made a pact with Zeus to never work as a seer again, so for the advice that I now give you, I do so as a friend who is repaying a personal debt.' He paused to gauge Jason's reaction. When satisfied he continued. 'To complete your quest, you must pass through the "Clashing Rocks" at the eastern side of the Bosporus. They are two small ironstone islands that are driven by the gods, without warning, to crush everything that passes between them. For the Argo to pass through them safely you must have impeccable timing. As you draw near, release a dove at the straights entrance, if it flies through successfully then, and only then, it will be safe for the Argo to sail through the passage.'

'Thank you, my friend.' The two men hugged in farewell. Jason boarded the ship and they raised the anchor and the Argo sailed east once more.

***

After several days the Argo did come to the ironstone islands that were situated in the waters below the Caynean Cliffs. The current was gentle, as was the breeze. The passage between the islands looked peaceful and inviting. Jason was initially tempted to simply sail on between them, but he called to Tiphys at the helm and ordered him to heave aside. Jason then ordered the sails to be taken down and the Argo slowed and drifted peacefully in the calm waters. They dropped anchor and held their station.

'Bring me the dove.' Jason commanded and Euphemus brought the caged bird onto the deck. Jason motioned to Euphemus that he should release the bird and the other Argonauts gathered to watch with anticipation as the bird headed due east and flew in a direct line between the rocky islands. Suddenly the rocks raced toward each other and clashed, the roar of the impact was deafening and frightening, and the Argonauts ducked their heads involuntarily. The sea wave spilled over the bow of the Argo and the crew were jostled uncomfortably. The rocks slowly parted and as the ship settled, the crew resumed searching for the dove. It was Euphemus that declared that the bird had passed through safely but that it appeared that it may have lost a few of its tail feathers. His crewmates laughed in relief.

Jason ordered the anchor raised and the sails hoisted. He then instructed Tiphys to steer the Argo through the gap between the rocks and they were almost through when the rocks rushed toward the stern of the ship. Jason feared the breeze was too weak to get them through fast enough so he roared the order to his men to row with all their strength. The Argo had managed to scrape past the rocks with only a heavy bump on the stern, and they managed to hold course and to continue onward. Several of the crew gasped in terror as they spied Tiphys lose his balance and fall overboard. They feared he was in danger of being crushed between the closing rocks. Some men rushed to the wheel and looked over the stern fearful that the sea below them would turn red. Then they saw Tiphys hanging onto a rope just above the waterline. He was laughing when they hoisted him up, and he quickly resumed his station at the tiller. Jason later inspected the minor damage to the rear of the ship and he remembered the lost tail feathers of the dove. He remonstrated himself for not properly heeding the omen. It was much later that Jason learned that due to the Argo's success in traversing the "Clashing Rocks," that they never clashed again. The Argo and her crew had removed the curse.

***

After two days of smooth sailing along the coast of the Black Sea, the Argo and her crew arrived at the mouth of the Acheron River and the home of the Mariandynians who were led by King Lycus. They all greeted Jason and the Argonauts warmly, and it turned out that news of the defeat and death of his enemy Amycus and his cronies of the Bebryces had preceded the Argo. King Lycus was jubilant and wanted to meet the champion that had killed Amycus with one blow. Polydeuces was pointed out by his crew mates and they yelled his praises as he stepped up to meet the king. After a night of feasting, the crew awoke and set about replenishing food and water stores. Some of the men were assigned hunting duties, but when they returned, Jason and the others were dismayed when they learned that Idmon, son of Apollo, had been slain by a wild boar. The other hunters had carried both Idmon, and the executed murderous beast, back to the Argo. It was agreed by all that they couldn't eat the boar, due to the grief that they felt for their deceased crew mate.

Several of the men became feverish from drinking brackish water. Two of the men recovered but Jason's close friend, Tiphys succumbed to the sickness and died. They constructed a funeral fire and mourned the deaths of the two men before setting sail once more. Lycus' son, Dascylus asked Jason to join his crew to which Jason agreed. He asked Ancaeus to take on the responsibility of steering the ship which he proudly accepted.

***

Several days later, they neared an island named Dia, an island that was sacred to Ares due to the shrine that was constructed on the island by the Amazons in his honour. The crew were suddenly pelted with arrow-like feathers from a flock of marauding birds. These birds of Ares, the Orniths Areioi, were there to protect the shrine. Many of the men were becoming inflicted with deep cuts and wounds, until Castor ordered his crew mates to raise shields to form a protective roof above their heads. With one hand they rowed, and with the other they held their shields, and in this way, they were slowly able to make it to shore. The men jumped ship, shouting and beating their shields with spears. Castor impulsively grabbed a horn and blew as hard as he could. The din that they made was enough to frighten and scatter the birds and temporarily drive them away from the island.

As they refreshed themselves and relaxed, they were approached by four shipwrecked survivors. They had been on the island for some time, but were unable to make a raft to escape, due to the constant barrage of the birds. Grateful that the Argonauts had driven the birds away, they appealed to Jason for rescue from this island prison. It turned out that the four men were sons of Phrixus, and they had been marooned whilst on a quest to recover their fathers Golden Fleece. The four brothers were named Argus, Phrontides, Melas and Cylindrus. Jason and the Argonauts listened with fascination as the four men told the account of their misfortunes. Jason concluded that they'd have some local knowledge of Aea, home of the Golden Fleece, and also that they would be better received by their grandfather, King Aeêtes, as his grandsons' rescuers. So, they fed and clothed them, and welcomed them aboard as part of his crew.

***

After several more days of sailing east, the Argo and her remaining crew finally arrived at Colchis, the home of the prized Golden Fleece.

As Argus was the eldest, and therefore the leader of the four brothers, he was their accepted spokesperson. He advised Jason to conceal the Argo near the mouth of the river Phasis, as it was an area that was never guarded. Jason agreed, as it would be terrible if their ship were impounded as soon as they arrived. Argus then persuaded Jason to remain with his men near the ship, whilst he and his brothers would discreetly fetch their mother, Chalciope. They were all confident that after learning of their rescue and of Jason's kindness toward them, that she too would want to assist Jason and his men.

Jason remained suspicious and on high alert. So, he had his men set up defensive positions surrounding the Argo. Both Castor and Polydeuces proved that they were naturals at organising the men. They strategically placed the men and ensured that enough weapons and supplies were at the ready, should they be attacked. They also sent men to be lookouts. The Argonauts remained vigilant, whilst they waited for news on how to proceed with the quest.

The four brothers however, were good to their word, and they soon returned with Chalciope and her much younger, and very beautiful sister, who was named Medea. Both were daughters of King Aeêtes. Chalciope was appreciative for the safe return of her four sons and she came to Jason and his crew with baskets of tasty treats and wine and made promises of much more when they entered the city.

It turned out that Medea was a powerful sorceress. She had the power of prophecy, and so had already known of Jason's arrival and the purpose of his quest. The prophecy she had received also told her that she'd fall in love with Jason, and that she would use her powers to assist him, even if it meant betraying her own father. Medea approached Jason and immediately applied her feminine charms in order to seduce him. Whilst Jason found Medea attractive, he determinately remained focused on his quest. He decided that he'd encourage her infatuation with him, as long as she assisted him to help achieve possession of the Golden Fleece.

Medea took his hand and led him away from the other Argonauts. After a short journey, they stepped under the shelter of a temple built in honour of Hera. She rounded him slowly whilst she caressed his muscular shoulders and arms. Medea leaned into him, her face moving near to Jason's. She spoke softly and seductively to him. 'I have followed your progress with much interest, Jason. You are obviously exceptionally skilled at many things.'

'I didn't realise that news of our voyage had travelled this far,' Jason replied and was genuinely surprised. He found himself enjoying the physical attention of an attractive female. It had been a long time since Lemnos.

'My father knows that you are here for the Golden Fleece, but he also fears that you are here to challenge him for his throne,' she informed him and then smiled. 'I explained to him that you have your own throne, and that it is waiting for you to claim, when you return home to Iolcus in Thessaly.'

'That's true. I only want the Golden Fleece, and I have no aspirations for his throne. I also presume that he won't give the fleece up easily,' Jason concluded. He smiled as he collected Medea's hand and kissed the back of it.

Medea blushed. She was pleased that her charms were evidently working on this handsome hero. 'I will assist you, but you must do as I say.'

'I'm grateful, and I will forever be in your debt,' Jason bowed. 'Your name will be known and you'll be honoured by all my people.' He then hesitated before adding. 'Why would you help me? It would be against the best interests of your own father.'

'But how will they know that it was me that helped you, if I was far away from them?' She connived, almost ignoring the question of her disloyalty toward her father. She stared deeply into Jason's eyes.

Jason understood the implication and so he quickly decided he'd invite her to join him. Smiling seductively, he asked, 'Perhaps you'd prefer to return to Iolcus with me, where we could expand on our emerging relationship.'

'Jason, the gods have already foretold that I will be your wife.' Medea smiled and then reached up to Jason and kissed him fully on his mouth. Jason reciprocated and their arms enveloped each other. Both were apparently enjoying the physicality of the embrace, and neither was displeased when Jason's groin revealed his amorous intent. She moved away from him, but looked happy and pleased. Her power and control of Jason was now established. 'We'll have time later to get better acquainted, but first we must plan your introduction to my father without the news of your arrival panicking him.'

Jason was becoming very pleased with all aspects of this new alliance. 'What do you suggest?'

'I will go to my father and arrange for you, and two of your men, to visit with him at his palace. I will persuade him that you come in peace and that as you are unarmed, that you have demonstrated your peaceful intentions. I will tell him that you are here for me, and that you desire the Golden Fleece as my wedding gift.'

'I don't think he'll believe that,' Jason said dismissively. 'He might believe that we have discovered an instant attraction for each other, but he would dismiss a pact of betrothal so soon after our arrival.'

Medea drew in a deep breath and sighed. She then looked up at him with a joyful expression as she'd had just thought of a solution. 'What if I was to tell him, that you and your men would agree to defeat his enemies, the Sauromatians? If you did that, he would want to handsomely reward you. You could then publicly claim the fleece as your payment, and he'd have to give it to you or he'd lose face and the respect from his subjects.' Medea loved her new plan and was wide eyed and excited as she explained it to him.

'Who are these Sauromatians?' Jason was doubtful about defeating an unknown enemy.

'They are nuisance raiders from the north. They sail across the black sea and steal our livestock and capture some of our women,' Medea explained. 'They mostly come at night, when the skies are clear and the moon is full. They are nomadic, so all of fathers attempts to find them and destroy them in their own lands have failed.'

'Perhaps...' Jason replied, the doubt evident in his voice. 'I'll visit with your father, I'm sure that he is already aware that we are here, and the reason why we have come to his kingdom. Perchance, he'll realise that he likes me, just as you have done.'

Medea moved nearer and hugged Jason. She turned her mouth to Jason's ear as she pressed her body hard against him. 'I doubt that very much,' she purred.

***

The following day, Jason and two of his trusted and respected Argonauts, ventured into the city and up to Aeêtes palace. They weren't challenged, but they were given an armed escort through the city and up to the palace gates. Here, they were handed over to palace guards and their journey continued into the palace itself. They entered a small room that seemed to adjoin the throne room. Next, Jason, along with Augeas and Telamon, were offered wine and cushions on which to sit and make themselves comfortable. They accepted the offered wine cups, but declined to sit down, preferring to be at the ready in case of trouble.

After a delay that stretched even Jason's patience, a messenger came to inform them that the king was now ready to receive them. Jason, Augeas, and Telamon, followed the man into the adjoining room. They found it peopled with armed guards, nobles, and King Aeêtes himself, seated on his highly polished metal throne, trying to look regal, but actually looking glum. His three visitors followed the servant who motioned them to stand before Aeêtes. They bowed in respect but said nothing, waiting to be spoken too, as was the practised custom.

'You have journeyed a great distance for a long time to fleece me of my most treasured prize.' Aeêtes spoke trying to make a joke out of Jason's plans. Jason and his crew mates smiled but said nothing. The tension within the room visibly reduced with Aeêtes own people grinning at the kings attempt at levity. 'Speak, Jason, Speak. It is why you are here.'

'May I introduce myself; I am Ja...'

'We know who you are!' Aeêtes roared. The room went quiet and some of the nobles turned pale and looked worried. Aeêtes then pointed to Jason's crew mates. 'Who are these two?'

'Ah.' Jason spied an opportunity. 'Allow me to introduce Augeas, son of Helios.' and Jason motioned in Augeas direction with an exaggerated bow. Augeas was about to respond by kneeling, but hesitated when Aeêtes screamed once more.

'I've never heard of either of them. Next!'

'This is Telamon. He is descended from Zeus himself,' Jason offered.

'It seems that half the world's people are somehow descended from Zeus. Perhaps that isn't such a big thing to brag about.' Aeêtes laughed and the others politely joined him with smiles and chuckles. Aeêtes had decidedly dismissed the second introduction as insignificant.

'How are you coping with the Sauromatian's these days?' Jason asked casually, hoping to get Aeêtes complete attention, and hopefully piquing his interest in doing a mutually beneficial deal.

'Well, I appreciate you asking. We're now doing better, all thanks to a deal I've recently struck with their king. My youngest daughter, Medea, has been promised in marriage to his eldest son. A stout, good-looking lad with a bit of an odour issue,' he explained smiling. 'The arrangement will encourage harmony and trade, and discourage further raids and acrimony.

The room went very still, as everyone heard a females coughing-fit and subsequent wailing from behind a curtain. Aeêtes smiled smugly. He had yet to personally inform his daughter about his disposition of her. Her gift of prophesy had evidently failed her on that one.

'I see...' Jason retorted, but plainly, he didn't have any idea what to say next. The pronouncement reinforced his plans to have Medea leave with him when he completed securing the fleece.

'I fear that my grandchildren may be aligning themselves to your cause,' Aeêtes nodded knowingly. 'I should be grateful to you for rescuing them, but in truth I was prepared for the probability of never seeing them again.'

Jason surmised that Aeêtes didn't have much respect or affection for his grandson's.

'I had hoped to do a trade for the Golden Fleece…' Jason decided to get straight to the point of his mission.

'You must understand that I'm in a bit of a bind about doing that,' Aeêtes replied wearily. 'You see, my reign as king of these parts, has been made dependant of my control and hold over the Golden Fleece. It is situated within the shrine of Ares, just in case you didn't know. If I lose it, or allow it to be stolen or destroyed, I must forgo my kingdom and well, I'd forfeit everything. So, you can comprehend my reluctance…'

Jason cut in. 'I'm in a bit of a difficult situation about the fleece myself. If I could simply reclaim…'

'Reclaim!' Aeêtes interrupted.

'Well, the Golden Ram was ours to begin with. Phrixus had no right to execute Chrysomallos and remove his fleece. My own claim on my own kingdom is dependent on my returning with the fleece.'

'Who is Chrysomallos?' Aeêtes demanded.

'That is the human name for the ram that grew the Golden Fleece. He is a son of Poseidon, and he rescued Phrixus from certain death,' Jason explained. 'He should have been honoured for his courage and bravery, and yet he was unfairly slaughtered.'

The nobles stirred restlessly. Some made motions to address the king. Aeêtes observed their discomfort and decided that he did not want this to happen with the Argonauts present. He cleared his throat and then announced, 'I will consult with my council and then we'll decide the fate of the Golden Fleece.'

Jason looked toward his two crew mates. They nodded in agreement and took this as a cue to retire from the king's audience. They performed a short respectful bow, turned, and left the chamber the way they had entered.

As they left the throne room, Jason, Augeas, and Telamon, were greeted by a valet and were invited to follow him. They were shown into a lavish room and were greeted by wait staff, who attended them with food, drink, clean clothes, a place to bathe, and beds on which to rest or sleep. They understood that they were forbidden to leave and they made no attempt to do so. They realised it would be rude to rattle the cage of a host that you hoped to draw benefit from.

The following morning after they had freshened up and breakfasted, they were escorted back into the throne room and stood once more before King Aeêtes. 'I trust you were well attended to?' he enquired politely.

'Thank you.' Jason bowed and the two others followed his example. 'You have been most generous.'

'I have given our conundrum much deliberation,' Aeêtes informed them, whilst looking at the council of nobles who had returned to be with the king to hear his pronouncement.

Jason noted that they looked tired, and it then occurred to him that they were wearing the same clothing as they had on the previous day. It must have been a protracted debate. Jason was tempted to ask for details but refrained. They'd know the fate of the Golden Fleece soon enough.

Aeêtes stood and addressed everyone present. 'The destiny of both of us as rulers of our kingdom's rests with our ownership of the Golden Fleece. It would seem that neither of us has an outright claim to it, but we both have been charged with possessing it for our own sake. Clearly in our case, there is no definitive solution.'

Jason was impressed. He feared that he would have to resort to trickery or theft, or perhaps even use force to liberate the Golden Fleece. The nobles had taken much into consideration and they perhaps felt that the king's claim was weak and in need of testing. 'You and your nobles have deliberated for some time about our conundrum. What do you have in mind?'

'I own two bulls. If you alone can harness both of them, and use them to pull a plough through a field, and then sow the seeds that I'll provide to you, then you can depart here with your crew on your ship with the fleece, and enough provisions to get you home. Furthermore, you'll do so as celebrated heroes of Colchis.' Aeêtes smiled, pleased with himself at the ease he'd felt describing this challenge.

Jason hesitated so Aeêtes continued. 'But if you refuse, then you and your closest men will be executed, and the remainder will be captured, beaten, and sold-off into slavery.'

Jason looked pensively at his two colleagues. They imperceptibly nodded their reply. He slowly turned to the king and spoke calmly. 'I'm eager to begin,' Jason replied, though he didn't sound like it.

'Good.' Aeêtes smiled and seemed pleased with himself. 'It is now up to the gods to determine your fate and our destiny.' He sat back down.

***

Jason and the others were once again escorted back to their resting room. After the servants departed, Medea entered the room through a panel on the side wall. Jason was startled as he hadn't initially recognised her, as she was dressed as a serving girl. He quickly recovered from his initial surprise, and was delighted when she came close to kiss and embrace him. She then spoke with urgent tones. 'My father is tricking you by making the challenge seem like a simple agricultural task; however, his bulls are enormous and powerful. They are so fierce that they have never been harnessed. They snort fire that burns people, and then stomp them to death with brazen hooves. These bulls are killers of humans, and now I'm so concerned for your safety.'

'How did he...' Jason tried to understand.

Medea explained the reason behind their power. 'They were a gift from Hephaestus and he mistakenly gave them strength that far exceeds common bulls.'

'Well, I have had some experience with ploughing...' Jason drew a deep breath and appeared to be somewhat overwhelmed.

'Jason, you do love me, don't you?' she smiled her most adorable feminine appealing smile, gently fluttering her eye lashes at him wide eyed with expectation.

'Of course, I do. My plan is to rescue you from that terrible forced marriage contract your father has ambushed you with. I will take you away from here to our new home as my bride.' He kissed her passionately to seal his commitment and she responded with equal passion.

As Medea broke free from their embrace, she beamed happily, almost dancing with enthusiasm. She suddenly stopped and looked seriously into his face as she explained. 'I can give you a potion that only the bulls can smell. It will pacify them long enough for you to harness the bulls and use them to plough a small field.'

'How do you know it is only a small field?' Jason was curious.

'My father never expects you to even harness the bulls, so the ploughing is almost incidental. It is the seeds that you must worry about.'

Jason drew a deep breath but said nothing.

'The seeds are the teeth from a dragon...'

'A dragon! Where did he get dragon teeth?' Jason was confused.

'They broke away from the dragon's mouth when he was defending the Golden Fleece from thieves.  When sown, they will form into the Sportoi, dead warriors from the underworld who will seek revenge for their early consignment to Hades. They are the fallen sons of Ares, and are therefore highly skilled warriors. They will be fierce, and angry about being disturbed. They will attack and try to kill you, Jason. Please my love, please defeat them,' Medea urged.

'I will,' he assured her, but he felt concern, and that he hadn't sounded convincing.

'Tomorrow, they'll collect you from your room, and take you to the field for the test of your cunning and strength. There, you'll prove your claim as the truthful owner of the Golden Fleece. But first, before you leave here, you must cover your body with this scented oil.' She handed him a large urn filled with the stuff. 'Use it to cover your whole body and apply it liberally on all your weapons. It will protect you from fire and from steel, and its odour will render the bulls docile.'

'Tell me about the dragon that guards the Golden Fleece? How do we deal with him?' Jason asked apprehensively, as he was grasping the enormity of the challenges before them.

'Now might be the right time for me to show you the path that you must use to get to the dragon's lair, after you have defeated the Sportoi warriors. I will deal with the dragon, so that you can liberate the fleece, and then we can flee to the Argo together,' Medea replied.

'Lead the way,' Jason agreed.

Medea walked to the concealed panel door, and Jason motioned to the two others that they should remain to guard the main door. They nodded in understanding and Jason followed Medea out of the room, down a dark stair well, and eventually out from under the palace. She held his hand as she guided him through the streets and passageways until they reached the shrine. It was a walled open-air enclosure, with sturdy metal bars at the front. The gates into the secured area were chained closed. In the middle of the compound, stood a cabinet with a glass front. Inside the cabinet was the Golden Fleece. Jason felt a little disappointed when he studied it. Legend spoke of its magnificence, but the fleece looked old and off colour. Jason next saw the dragon. Fortunately, it was much smaller than he'd imagined.

'Don't be fooled by his size,' Medea warned sensing his surprise at the monster's smallish proportions. 'He is a vicious killer and no-one will go near him.'

'How do we...?' Jason was confused.

'By the time you get here, the dragon will be asleep. You alone will free the fleece from its mount and together we will make haste for the Argo,' she explained.

Jason looked fondly at Medea. His love and respect for her grew more each moment they were together. She led him down another short path that took them to the fields that he had to plough. Jason was now confident that he'd find his way to the dragon cage. They next returned to the palace, all the while remaining unseen from her father's men. At the entrance to the concealed passage back to his room, she kissed him fondly and departed. Jason then scrambled in the dark and returned to his room.

***

The following day, the three men were escorted from the palace by an armed guard. Jason felt weird covered from head to toe with the oil. Augeas smiled and assured him that he smelled pretty, and not to concern himself. 'Focus on the challenge and the prize,' he advised. We'll soon leave this place with the fleece, and you with a bride.'

Jason smiled his acknowledgment. Telamon dutifully carried the remaining oil and they hoped they'd get the opportunity to re-oil their weapons before the trial commenced.

The field was small. It was adjoined by a pen that held the two bulls that seemed docile as they munched happily on a bale of hay. The field to be ploughed was at the foot of a hill on which it seemed the entire population of Colchis, who were assembled to watch these bulls burn and trample Jason to his death for his foolish quest. Outside the bull's pen they returned Jason's weapons to him. Augeas and Telamon made a show of inspecting and cleaning the weapons when they were actually giving them a protective coating of Medea's oil.

Aeêtes held up his hands and the crowd roared its approval at being present to witness this magnificent trial of bravery and strength. Their only concern was that it would be over too soon. Jason held a sword up high to acknowledge the crowd, and to indicate his willingness to undertake these trials and earn his prize. He didn't wait to be told to start. He casually approached the bull pen, opened the gate and stepped inside. The bulls were momentarily distracted from eating by the roar of the crowds, but they soon recovered and became angry and aggressive, their eyes glowed a fierce red, and they clearly wanted to burn and gore Jason for his intrusion. Jason stood his ground and made a show of lowering his sword before them, as he realised that the pheromone from the oils had started to take effect.

To the amazement of the king, the nobles, the guards and the crowds, Jason was able to pacify the bulls by simply placing the palm of his hands on each of their foreheads. The bulls resumed eating as Jason carefully lifted the harnesses off the rail and gently tied it over each of the now peaceful bulls. He next attached the plough, and he gently motioned to the bulls that they should pull. They did so and walked calmly as they quickly turned the soil into long furrows.

The crowd watch on in stunned silence, but Aeêtes sensed trickery. He was about to intercede when the nobles ordered the senior guards to restrain him. They stood behind Aeêtes, and so he decided to sit down, relax, smile, wave to the crowd, and continued watching the event.

After about thirty minutes, the field was completely ploughed, and Jason carefully returned the bulls to their pen. There he gently unharnessed them, all the time whispering calmly to them and gently caressing them to keep them peaceful. After securing the gate to the bull pen, he commenced the next phase, the task of planting the dragon's teeth. From a cloth bag he dropped the teeth into the soil, covering each as he went. As soon as he finished, the soil began to stir beneath him. Giant skeletal warriors magically rose up from the soil, brandishing swords, spears, and shields. They shook loose the soil from their bones and looked about in surprise. They then saw Jason who was also armed and clearly ready to fight them. They formed up into a fighting formation, and poised their weapons ready to charge him. They were completely surprised when Jason dropped his sword and shield, and picked up a giant rock that had been released from the soil through ploughing. He hurled it into the skeletal army, smashing bones, and causing the dead warriors to crash into each other.

Jason's audience roared in approval. The skeletal warriors jostled, and some even started engaging each other with their swords, with several falling down disassembled and defeated. The closest warriors resumed attacking Jason, and so he threw more rocks at them from a pile that Telamon and Augeas had tossed together. When the rock supply was exhausted, he gathered his sword and shield, and courageously fought them off. Some only lost a bone or two when he struck them, and they were able to continue fighting. Others totally fell apart, and remained fallen.

It took Jason many duels to finally defeat all of the Sportoi. As soon as it became clear that he would be victorious, the crowd roared respect each time he dispatched one of them. Jason had now completed the unimaginable, and he had earned his right to claim the Golden Fleece.

Breathing heavily, and totally exhausted from battle, he turned to Aeêtes to see if he was ready to concede to his victory, but to his surprise Aeêtes was gone. The nobles and guards who were also mesmerised by Jason's skills, strength, and ultimate victory over the bulls and the Sportoi warriors, had also failed to notice Aeêtes discrete departure.

Jason bowed to the jubilant crowds and left the field of bones. He, along with Augeas and Telamon, headed swiftly for Ares sacred grove and the temple that was guarded by a sleepless dragon. To his surprise he saw Castor on the path and he encouraged Jason to keep running. 'I'm here with Polydeuces and five other men,' he explained as he ran with Jason. 'We'll delay the Colchian soldiers while you retrieve the fleece.'

'How's the Argo?' Jason asked as they ran.

'The crew have replenished the ship, and we're ready to set sail as soon as we're all onboard.'

'That's great!' Jason was pleased.

They arrived where Polydeuces, Meleager and the other heavily armed Argonauts were ready to defend the path. Castor broke free from the run and joined the others as Jason, Augeas and Telamon continued to fetch the Golden Fleece. When they arrived, they found Medea had rendered the dragon into a deep sleep. She had also managed to unlock the gate. Jason grinned at her with admiration as he raced in, leapt over the beast, smashed the cabinet, bundled the Golden Fleece under his arm, and then jumped back to safety, just as a snake lunged out at Jason's retreating feet.

'What the...' Jason was startled.

'I'm sorry, Jason,' Medea said and looked distressed. 'I did not know about the snake.'

'No matter,' Jason assured as he kissed her. 'We have the Fleece and I am unharmed,' he said and smiled warmly to comfort her. Then the four of them turned and raced for the Argo.

When Jason had surprisingly defeated the Sportoi, Aeêtes' soldiers floundered without their king to yell out his commands. It took them some time to rally, and the Argonauts only encountered token resistance, as they followed Jason and Medea back to the Argo.

As they drew nearer to the ship, Polydeuces started yelling to the crew to raise the anchors and hoist the sails. By now, their pursuers had mustered and were close behind them. They raced up the boarding plank which was immediately raised when they were all onboard. Oarsmen pushed the ship away from the shore and into the breeze, and they dipped their oars and pulled. The Argo's sail caught the wind and they were now on their way.

A smaller vessel began its pursuit of the Argo. On board were Aeêtes most loyal officers and men. The boat was powered by strong oarsmen, and on deck were soldiers armed with bows and arrows. They aimed high and commenced a barrage of arrows raining down on the Argonauts. It was then that Apsyrtus, Medea's much younger brother revealed himself. He had stowed on board hoping to remain with the sister he adored and escape from the father he feared. To Jason's surprise, Medea grabbed her brother and held him in front of her, in full view of their pursuers. Immediately upon seeing him, the bowman lowered their bows fearing they would inflict a mortal wound on their king's favoured heir to his throne. The Argo was now increasing its speed, but the other ship was slowly gaining on them. Jason was again startled when his beloved pushed her brother off the ships side and into the deep-sea water. 'My father's men will have to heave aside to rescue him. They dare not let him drown as my fathers' wrath will be unending,' she explained, clearly pleased with her quick-thinking actions.

The pursuers did drop sail and rowed in reverse to slow the boat. Jason watched as they struggled to hoist the near drowned boy from the water. The Argo was now aided by a strong sea current and a strong easterly wind. 'Raise oars!' he commanded when they were clearly well away from their pursuers and danger.

***

The lengthy journey home to Iolcus was mostly uneventful. The Argonauts were desperate to get home to their wives and to their kingdoms. The stories that were told of their return journey were distorted over the years, with many regions falsely claiming that the Argonauts had visited them, so that they could share in some of the glory with the stories numerous re-tellings.

They later learned that the men sent by Aeêtes to go after them were promised terrible retribution by their king, should they return without Medea and the Golden Fleece. Wisely, they collectively chose to not pursue the Argo, or return to Cochis, preferring a safer life in a different land. The crew of the Argo encountered some obstacles and challenges on the return journey, but these were minor compared to those they experienced on route to Cochis and the Golden Fleece.

One of these incidents was when they were sailing too close to the rocks at Charybdus, after being lured toward them by the Sirens enchanting songs. Orpheus was able to break their spell with his loud singing of a counter melody. Many of the crew joined him and the intense situation became quite comical. The Argo sailed on and away from the danger. As Peleus looked overboard, he thought he'd spied his beloved Thetis guiding the Argo away from danger. He smiled at the thought of her, and he waved at the water and imagined that the sea had waved back at him. He had missed her terribly and hoped that she'd be there to greet him when they finally got back to Iolcus.

***

When the Argo finally neared the city of Iolcus they encountered a violent storm. A freak wave carried the Argo inland and they became grounded. After the storm dissipated, they were met on the beach by a furious Herakles. Without a word, he slit the throats of both Zetes and Calais for their part in abandoning him at Mysia. He was about to do the same to Jason, when Castor and Polydeuces stepped in-between them. Herakles allowed them to restrain him as he had much respect and friendship for the twins.

The looks they gave each other confirmed what they had already suspected about the deceit, and subsequent desertion of their crew mates.

'Jason was misled by Zetes and Calais, and you had every right to dispatch them,' Castor explained to an indignant Herakles. He looked at Jason and Polydeuces for support and they both nodded vigorously.

Polydeuces added, 'Jason didn't know what to do. He was assured by Glaucus that you had abandoned our crew and the quest. He said that you had decided to return to Greece to complete your tasks.'

Herakles started to visibly relax. He now fully understood how Jason came to that conclusion and why he ordered the Argo to sail off without him. 'Zetes and Calais tried to thwart me many times.'

'I apologise for my error, Herakles. Please, forgive me,' he bowed, and he looked at Herakles for a sign. He saw the man relax, and so he continued. 'You will have your full share of the spoils, and you will also receive the shares of Zetes and Calais,' Jason offered. He was keen to appease this giant of a man and right the wrongs of leaving him behind.

'Herakles, please accept his offer, as the bounty has been plentiful. You'll be wealthy.' Castor smiled at his friend and then hugged him into submission.

As he broke free from Castor's embrace, he proclaimed, 'I agree!' Herakles roared smiling. The others cheered in approval.

'Please tell me, what became of Eurtion?' Jason asked.

Herakles sighed. He looked furtively at the others. 'It seems that in his hunger, he ate a dead animal, and… it sickened him,' he explained and nodded slowly. 'He suffered in much agony,' Herakles added with evident sadness in his voice.

The others nodded, but said nothing. Hunger makes for poor judgments.

'I'm going to say hello to the others,' Herakles said and turned and walked away, now satisfied with his promised compensation.

Jason turned to Castor and Polydeuces. 'The two of you have contributed much to our success and are deeply respected by me and the Argonauts. Without the two of you my quest would have failed. I owe you a great debt.'

'We are honoured to have been invited to join you. Orpheus has composed many songs and stories that tell our tale of adventure and glory. They are bound to become very popular,' Castor explained.

'And, you could pay us,' Polydeuces added.

Jason smiled. 'I'm now about to inherit my father's kingdom. As a direct result of securing the Golden Fleece, I will become a wealthy man,' he said smiling happily before continuing. 'As owner of the

Argo, I get three shares. As Captain, I get an additional three shares.' Jason placed his hands on the twins' shoulders. 'I have decided that I want you both to have my shares. You will each get four shares.' Jason smiled, happy with his decision. 'You may need to buy a donkey to help you carry it all,' he added and grinned.

Castor and Polydeuces were now heavily burdened with gold and coin as they had received their share of the spoils. They returned home to their wives and children, filled with glorious stories of the challenges they encountered when they sailed with Jason on the Argo to claim the Golden Fleece.

***

Thetis and Peleus were now happily reunited. She surprised him with the introduction of a young adult male. 'His name is Achilles,' she told him proudly. 'And, he is your son.'

Peleus wasn't surprised at his size, as he was well aware of a demigod's ability to grow rapidly into adulthood. He bid his farewell to Jason and his crew mates, and then he and Thetis set off to Mount Olympus to be married. Little did anyone realise that an oversight that occurred as a result of their wedding would become the spark that started a war between the Greeks and the Trojans.

Their own son, Achilles became a fierce warrior and a key figure in that war, and he fought bravely against the Trojans of Troy, but sadly he died in battle.

***

In the months and years that followed their return to Iolcus, Medea had to again use her trickery to finally depose Pelias and secure the throne for Jason. His followers were pleased with the Golden

Fleece, but they were disappointed with Jason's marriage to Medea. After their initial happiness, it developed into an unhappy union. As Medea was a foreigner, she was believed by many to be unworthy and untrustworthy.

They fought often, and their union only lasted ten years, ending in divorce when Jason fell in love with another better suited woman.

***

Many years before Jason and his crew set off on the quest for the Golden Fleece, Zeus had indulged in an affair with his cousin, a Titan named Leto. Hera was upset and angry when she discovered that her husband had once again betrayed her trust. It infuriated her even more when she learned it was done by mutual consent, and that it required no use of trickery on her husband's part. As often was the case with Zeus, Leto was with child, and she was having twins. Hera enacted an agonisingly painful pregnancy and difficult childbirth on Leto as punishment for having sex with her husband. She wanted to set an example and use her suffering as a warning to all others. Their daughter was delivered first and she was named Artemis. Her place of birth was Ortygia on the east coast of the island of Sicily, but the midwives were warned by Hera, "Do not allow the birth of her second baby on your island, or you will face my wrath."

So, the frightened midwives drugged poor Leto to delay the birth of the second baby. She left Ortygia by boat, but Leto was denied assistance wherever she landed. Nine days later, Leto had travelled more than a thousand kilometres farther east to Delos, where it was Eileithyia, goddess of childbirth and the daughter of Hera and Zeus, who showed her kindness and mercy. She defied her mother and assisted Leto with the baby's delivery. After much agony, Artemis' twin brother Apollo was finally born.

***

Zeus grew affectionate toward these twins, and he particularly favoured his daughter. He loved to grant Artemis many gifts and grant her special powers. When she was three, she asked her father for a bow and quiver with an unlimited supply of perfectly made arrows. She decided she wanted to be goddess of the mountains, which Zeus granted, as they were her home and her hunting grounds. She asked that only one city honour her, as she shunned duties as a goddess. But Zeus was too generous and gave her thirty cities and arranged for their inhabitants to erect shrines in honour of her. He also made her the guardian of roads and harbours. Lastly, she vowed to her father that she'd remain a virgin. Whilst this request would not have been one of Zeus' own desires, he was resolved to assist her in achieving it.

She became known as the goddess that fiercely protected both her virginity and her nudity. As the goddess of the hunt, she was happiest when running through the forests with her virgin nymphs. She enjoyed the kill, but she was also the protector of young creatures, and this may have given cause to the moral position of only killing and eating mature animals that remains true today. She was rarely seen without her bow and arrows, and she wore only hunting clothes. She was close friends with Selene, goddess of the moon, and Atalanta, a swift footed and highly skilled huntress. She often hunted at night and in their company.

Due to her mother's experience with the painful birth of Apollo, she also became a goddess of childbirth and a protector of women in labour. However, she could also be malevolent and would bring about sickness, and even death, to any person when she was personally offended by them. Sadly, for some, Artemis was easily offended, and was known to enact revenge on anyone who dared cross her, or lose her favour.

If she was observed by mortals, she would sometimes become angry. If she was out-rightly insulted by mortals, she would enact fierce retribution. So, many decades later when King OEneus of Calydon, a region famous for its wine production, failed to honour her properly and include her in their annual harvest sacrifices, she sent them the biggest, meanest, most ferocious, wild boar imaginable to terrorise him and the people of Calydon.

The boar bristled with spikes the size of spears and its tusks were the size of the tusks of a grown elephant. It had razor sharp teeth and damaging hooves. Its eyes blazed a fiery red, and its foul foamy breath burned fire. It was alert, fast, agile, tremendously strong, and determinately aggressive.

King OEneus was devastated and he quickly appealed to Artemis to be allowed to make restitution, but for him it was too late, as she had already loosed the boar, and set it on its path of destruction. It trampled crops, uprooted vines, and pushed down the olive trees. Flocks of domesticated birds scattered, and herds of livestock stampeded in terror of its approach. Many were killed. Even the king's officers and warriors were too frightened to deal with the beast. The Calydonian farmers fled to the protection of their city's walls, and soon they were running low on food.

OEneus' son Meleager had recently returned home a hero, having been a part of Jason success in the quest for the Golden Fleece. He was proven to be brave, schooled, and also well trained and now experienced in the arts of fighting and weaponry. OEnues and his wife Althea were justifiably proud of their son, and they felt confident that he was fit to one day inherit the throne.

Both OEneus and Meleager personally knew many of the heroes and famed warriors of the Greek world. They sent urgent dispatches to call upon them to help their people kill this beast, and rid them of this terror. The hunt came to be known as the Great Calydonian Boar Hunt. It was the second time in Greek mythical history that heroes from all over Greece were united to deal with a formidable foe.

Many warriors responded and they each managed to sneak past the boar to enter the city via the strong city gates. The first to arrive was Jason. He was now famous as the warrior who had successfully captained a journey with his crew of Argonauts and reclaimed the missing Golden Fleece. Meleager had been a valued Argonaut and when he had made the call, Jason and many of the other former Argonauts, quickly answered, their comradery still strong.

Ancaeus next arrived carrying his famous massive two headed axe. Also, with them came Hippothous, Eurypylus, Iphicles, Nestor, Lynceus, Telamon, Peleus and Mopsus. Eurtion surprised many by showing up. Herakles hadn't known if he had survived the food poisoning and none had heard from him since their return to Iolcus. He was warmly welcomed by all.

The next day, Theseus, a famous hero who had killed the Minotaur, and the Crommyonian Sow, had agreed to join the hunt and he was warmly greeted by the other warriors when he arrived at Calydon. Iolaus, the famed nephew of Herakles arrived, but he was without his hero uncle. Herakles had decided not to join them as he needed to complete the list of tasks in order to lift his curse.

Both Castor and Polydeuces arrived at the city, having answered the call. They were now also counted amongst the gathered brave hunters. They were healthy, fit, strong, and ready for the challenge. Both of Meleager's uncles, brothers to his mother Althea, were present and eager to join the hunt. Uncle Toxeus was a skilled archer, and his brother Uncle Plexippus, was skilled with the javelin.

The most surprising warrior who offered her skills to the hunt, was Atalanta. She was previously rejected by Jason in her desire to join the quest for the Golden Fleece, but here she was, presenting herself for inclusion in the hunt for the boar. She was known to be a close friend of Artemis, and so many believed she was sent by the Goddess to torment the male warriors who wouldn't approve of a woman as one of the hunters. Meleager was again smitten by her. He still hadn't married, and he became resolved to impress her with his own leadership and hunting skills. Atalanta remembered Meleager's previous attraction toward her, but again she did nothing to encourage him. Her vow of virginity, her disinterest in sex, and in all men in general, had remained unchanged.

The hunters were gathered within the safety of the city walls. OEneus stood proudly beside his son as Meleager laid out his plans for the actual hunt. Meleager spoke confidently when he addressed the assembled brave men and the one woman who'd undertake the actual search and destruction of the nemesis of Calydon.

'These swift runners will soon be dispatched in each direction,' he explained pointing to a group of young and athletic men. They wore only loin cloth and running sandals. Each man was painted in shades of green and brown so as to camouflage them in the trees and shrubs to help them to avoid the attention of the beast. 'They each carry a torch that when lit will give off bright red smoke,' Meleager continued. 'They will seek out the current location of the boar, scale a tree, light the torch, thus signalling to us where we will start the hunt.'

The hunters looked at the runners with a mixture of pity and respect.

'Why has Atalanta been allowed to join our ranks?' Eurypylus questioned, his hostility was clearly in his voice. He glared at Atalanta who was unperturbed by his malice.

'She has volunteered, and she has the necessary skill attributes required to make a contribution,' Meleager defended. This time, he was in charge, and the decision to include her was his alone to make.

'Eurypylus, are you worried about being bested by a girl?' Hippothous teased.

'She is no match for a man,' Eurypylus retorted pointing to Atalanta dismissively.

'Still, she might be a distraction to us real hunters. She should remain here, safe within the city walls,' Iphicles advised.

'If you focus on the task, she'll be no more a distraction to you than any other warrior.' Meleager was getting annoyed by this unnecessary diversion from discussing his strategy.

Toxeus, and his brother Plexippus, studied each other and nodded in agreement. Toxeus often spoke for both of them. 'We agree that there should be no women hunters.'

Hippothous decidedly agreed with Meleager. 'If she is no match for us, or if she becomes fearful, then she'll quickly return to the city of her own accord. We are all experienced, and so let us focus on the task, and not worry ourselves about her gender.'

Many murmured their support for Hippothous words, but Eurypylus and Iphicles moved over to stand with Meleager's uncles in a show of solidarity.

Jason, now king of Iolcus, stepped forward to speak. He was comfortable with his role as a leader, but he was also mindful that he was here as a guest of OEneus' and his son Meleager. 'I say let her run and let her hunt with us. It can do no harm and besides, she'll be able to recount the story of our victory with far greater skill than any of us.' The resultant laughter eased some of the tension that was manifesting.

Meleager stared at Jason with concern. He had found himself still having some desire for Atalanta despite her reputation for having no interest in developing relationships. He knew of the tragedy that was Jason's marriage to Medea and now hoped he didn't have competition from Jason for her favours. Meleager sided up to Jason, placed his hands on his shoulders and declared. 'Spoken like a confident warrior.' This had the immediate effect of neutralising further dissention, as to do so would make any dissenter look weak.

OEneus next stepped forward and held his hands high up to attract everyone's attention. 'You all do us proud to be here with us in our time of great need. Your names will reverberate in history for what you are about to achieve. Unfortunately, we have limited wealth and each of you will only be modestly rewarded for your participation. I can offer the warrior that is responsible for the kill, to be awarded the boars pelt and tusks as a trophy. That boar has killed so many, and I worry about having to ask you to risk your lives, to save others from that fate. I wish that I could offer you more, and I fear that some of you might not return. May the gods be merciful and take care of you.'

'Here, here,' was the collective response.

'Where are your hunting dogs?' someone asked.

'They are dead,' Meleager answered. 'All of them were killed by the beast, along with many of my soldiers.'

Meleager continued addressing the hunters and he detailed his plan to them. 'We'll divide into three teams. I'll lead the first group, with Jason leading the second, and Theseus the third.' Both Jason and Theseus broke away and those who felt comfortable under their respective leaderships drifted away with them.

The first group of hunters comprised of Meleager, Atalanta, Eurypylus, Iphicles, Lynceus, and Mopsus.

Meleager looked overly pleased that Atalanta had decided to join him in his team. The others looked worried about this and hoped that he wouldn't become too distracted from their purpose by her presence. Meleager next detailed what each team would do. 'My team will exit the city through the gate and head straight down the main road in full view from the forests. We may be able to draw out the beast and that would be a good outcome as it'll be easier to engage the animal in the open field.'

The second group comprised of Jason, Ancaeus, Castor, Polydeuces, Nestor, and Hippothous.

'Jason. After leaving the city wall you'll lead your team away to the left of the main road and take up a covered position near the stables.'

In the third group was Theseus, Toxeus, Plexippus, Eurtion, Peleus, Iolaus, and Telamon.

'Theseus, your group will turn right from the gate and head toward the vineyard barns. Remember everyone, be watchful of the red signal smoke, as that will indicate that a runner has located the boar. If you hear that one of the teams has engaged the animal, I want the other two teams to converge on their position and reinforce them.'

'Do you think it'll take more than one team to prevail?' Theseus asked expressing his surprise.

'I do,' Meleager replied. They all stood still in silence, each hunter in deep thought mentally preparing for their encounter with the dangerous beast.

So, without ceremony, farewells, or well wishes, the three groups headed out through the city gates to their designated starting points, ready to commence hunting the dreaded animal.

***

Soon the red smoke was spotted. It was to the left of the gate, beyond the stables, and it was Jason and his team who raced toward it in pursuit of glory. As they approached a thicket, they heard sounds of the boar ramming a tree. The boar was clearly unconcerned with their approach, focusing on the tree. The hunters looked up to see a frightened runner that had climbed high up in the trees upper branches in order to escape the boar. The boar turned and snorted at the hunters, undaunted by their numbers or weapons. The flames and smoke emanating from its snout soon clouded the hunter's view.

Nestor launched his spear at the beast, but it fell short. Ancaeus laughed as he raised his two headed axe above his head. 'I'll show you all how to kill a boar,' Ancaeus boasted, as he raced through the smoke. To his surprise, his foot fell into a hollow in the ground and he fell heavily, rolling on the dirt, landing with his back to the beast. The boar launched itself at Ancaeus thrusting its tusks into him, the first piercing his upper thigh as the other tusk burst out through his abdomen. The boar violently shook his victim, and Ancaeus guts exploded with a red bloody mist as his insides spewed out, flung across the ground in a wide arc. The others held back from launching their weapons, either traumatised from what was happening, or in fear of striking Ancaeus.

The boar withdrew, blood staining its tusks. It turned and ran off, away from the shocked group of men. Their energy was instantly spent, and they were quiet for a moment while they breathed heavily slowly gathering their composure. After a brief pause, Nestor collected his spear and picked up the axe. They looked at each other, nodded, and calmly resumed tracking the boar following its trail left by heavy hoof prints.

As they walked, they discussed what had happened. Jason spoke first. 'I think we wasted an opportunity to kill the boar, we should have struck when its tusks were restrained by Ancaeus.'

Castor and Polydeuces had so far contributed little to the hunt and were deeply disturbed by Ancaeus sudden and brutal death. 'We vow to avenge him.' Castor said looking at his brother, his voice conveying sorrow that they had done nothing but watch Ancaeus being killed. They walked in silence as they followed Jason through the forest. These pursuers had temporarily lost track of the boar.

***

The group led by Theseus saw a line of red smoke rising across the skyline. He and his team watched and were surprised at how quickly new columns of smoke emerged. The boar was travelling swiftly and heading east. The gathered group plotted a possible interception point and then they hurriedly set off, hoping to converge with the beast and claim the kill. After crossing a cornfield, they stealthily entered a thicket, planning to surprise the boar and have the advantage. They walked towards an enormous tree. Theseus motioned to his men that they should separate into two groups to circle around the tree. As they did, there was a sudden movement on the side of the tree where Peleus, Iolaus, and Telamon were walking. Iolaus and Telamon raised their swords and Peleus raised his javelin ready to launch, just as a frightened cow emerged from the brush, snorting and grunting in fear. The others had now rounded the tree and saw the men, weapons ready, poised to attack a harmless domestic beast. They collectively sighed, laughed, and visibly relaxed. Iolaus slapped the cow on its rump and it bellowed before racing into the clearing.

'Look for red smoke,' Theseus commanded and his team looked upwards but saw nothing, the tree canopy blocking their view.

'I'll climb a tree and have a look,' Plexippus suggested.

As Toxeus and Eurtion assisted Plexippus up the difficult part of the trunk of a climbable tree, the others watched in all directions providing a defensive shield to the three men.

'Smoke!' Plexippus called out as soon as he was half way up the tree. The others looked up and saw him pointing to the west. They turned in preparation for an attack.

'Come down,' Theseus ordered. They waited until Plexippus was once more on the ground and they then headed in a westerly direction with their weapons poised at the ready. It didn't take them very long to locate the savage boar. It charged into them, belching fire and smoke. Peleus raised his javelin and launched it with all his might toward the beast. Sadly, the javelin missed the boar but struck his close friend Eurtion in his chest, instantly killing him. The boar twisted out of the path of others drawn swords, but its razor-sharp bristles brushed past Telamon and he was savagely wounded by them, blood gushing from multiple injuries. The boar ran on, turned toward the brush, and escaped the remaining men.

'It's just a scratch,' Telamon assured them as he reviewed his wounds.

Theseus examined Telamon. 'You're out of this hunt. Return to the city and get help,' Theseus concluded. Telamon looked deeply into Theseus's eyes, saw his concern and he conceded with a nod.

Peleus had broken down and now openly wept as the others gently extracted his javelin from Eurtion's body. They had all become very quiet at the sudden death of one of their team. They hadn't as yet, inflicted any wounds on the animal they pursued. They wiped the blood away from the weapon and offered it to Peleus, but he refused to take it.

'You'd both better head back to the city gates,' Theseus advised him, his voice heavy with compassion.

'Shall I...?' Iolaus was about to suggest that he accompany them when Peleus cut him off.

'No.' I'm fine. Just give me a moment and then I'll be ready to kill this monster.' Peleus stood up and took the once again proffered javelin. 'I'll come back for his body after the boar is dead.'

Iolaus assisted the badly wounded Telamon back to Calydon. They had crudely bound his wounds, and Iolaus hoped they could get to help before his friend bled out.

The others drew a deep breath and they headed off, with some haste, in a westerly direction intent on finding and destroying the savage boar.

***

Meanwhile in Meleager's group, the bickering about Atalanta's presence continued. They had been wandering in and out of thickets for a long time. Their direction altering each time someone spied a fresh column of red smoke, but they were no closer to seeing, let alone finding or killing the beast.

Meleager was getting impatient with the constant barrage of insults that Eurypylus's had directed at Atalanta. He complained about how she would slow them down when it mattered, and that a woman had no place being with them. Atalanta had shown no signs of being bothered by Eurypylus feelings about her. She often attracted this type of negativity, and had long ago learned to ignore it. She smiled at Meleager reassuringly, but he misunderstood the gesture, and took it to be a silent plea for him to do more to stop the harassment.

Eurypylus was about to speak once more, when Meleager turned and drew his sword and held the point against the man's throat. He was angry and wanted him to know it. 'Eurypylus! Would you please shut up and deal with the fact that Atalanta is here and is one of us. She is here at my invitation, with my full support, and has my respect as a skilled, capable hunter.'

Iphicles interceded on his friend's behalf. 'Meleager! For the love of the gods, please just send Atalanta back to the safety of the city, and let us men get on with killing this animal. Fighting amongst ourselves does nothing to help your people.'

Meleager's anger rose significantly. Having to deal with Eurypylus' infuriating behaviour was bad enough, and now Iphicles was joining in also. Meleager swung his sword arm in a wide ark to transfer his threatening blade to this new nuisance, but he misjudged the distance. Instead of arriving under the man's chin, he actually slit his throat. Blood poured from the wound, and Iphicles was dead before his body fell to the ground. Eurypylus screamed out in shock, but Meleager's blood lust was now active, and he took the cry to be a charge and drove his sword into Eurypylus' abdomen and up into his heart. He too fell to the ground dead.

If Atalanta felt any emotion, she chose not to show it. It could have been that she was pleased her tormenters were dispatched. She may have been impressed with Meleager's sword skill. Or, she may have feared being his next target if she said anything. It could have been that death was a natural conclusion for all warriors and hunters, and so she took it in her stride. Meleager however, took her indifference as approval, and smiled at her as he calmly wiped his sword blade on the recently murdered man's clothing.

Lynceus and Mopsus wisely chose to say nothing. Inwardly, they were terribly shocked by what they had just witnessed. Lynceus looked deeply into Mopsus' eyes, but he could read nothing in them. They both drew in a deep breath and scoured the area for any signs of red smoke so that they could continue the hunt and leave this tragedy behind them.

'There,' Mopsus said as he pointed toward a thick column of red smoke. Soon the four remaining hunters were on the move. After a extended march, they entered a clearing where they found the other two groups gathered, positioning themselves for the kill.

'We've cornered the beast into this canyon.' Jason explained to Meleager as the three hunting teams united into one group.

Meleager asked his two team captains. 'How have you fared against the beast?'

'One fallen,' Jason replied.

'One fallen, and one badly wounded. A third is taking him to the city for medical help,' Theseus answered.

'We have lost two,' Meleager reported. 'Has anyone managed to wound the beast?' he asked.

Looking at their faces, Meleager had his answer.

'Let's set up the nets in case the beast manages to get past us,' Meleager ordered.

Each team had carried a large trapper's net folded in a pack which was carried on a volunteer's back. Castor and Polydeuces took charge of positioning the nets and the work was quickly and efficiently completed. The plan was to stretch them across the mouth of the canyon in the hope that it would entangle the beast if it managed to get passed them, as they closed in on its position.

They next spread themselves out covering the width of the pass into the canyon. At Meleager's hand gesture, they all advanced cautiously deeper into the canyon and hopefully, into glory. After many minutes of walking and slowly drawing in nearer to each other as the canyon narrowed, they could hear the squeals of the cornered boar. They could tell that the animal was exhausted from fleeing and that it knew it was trapped. They watched as the boar attempted to climb the steep sides of the canyon's walls, and they watched it fall down heavily onto the ground.

When the boar saw the hunters, its red eyes blazed both in fear and in hatred. Its foamy mouth shot out fire and thick smoke and then it charged. The boar was heading straight for Castor, Polydeuces, and Lynceus. The three formed a Spartan defensive movement by crouching down, spears thrust forward with the shaft end embedded into the ground. If the beast continued it would impale itself on the three spears and they would not let it pass them. The boar saw the threat in time and managed to veer away. Atalanta was in the right position and launched her spear at the boar's right flank. The head of the spear managed to penetrate the hide and a wound opened, blood pouring out from it. The boar completed its turn and retreated back into the canyon. Theseus let loose his spear, but he only managed to impale a tree. Jason also launched his weapon, but he also missed.

'First blood!' Meleager shouted excitedly. 'Atalanta has drawn first blood.' He was clearly pleased it was her that succeeded in doing it. It achieved so many things including vindicating his decision to have her with them, as well as doing more to earn his admiration.

The others could see that it was a mere flesh wound, and that it wouldn't impede the animal, but they chose not to say anything. On Meleager's signal they continued to advance. They rounded the bend and came nearer to the end of the canyon. The beast charged once more and tried to circumnavigate the hunters by running up the embankments in an attempt to race past them, but the walls were too steep, and so it turned into Mopsus impaling him. This action slowed the boar sufficiently for Meleager to slit the boar's throat with a killing stroke of his sword. Mopsus bled out in front of the remaining hunters who were powerless to save their friend as his wounds were far too severe. They stood and watched in silence, panting and exhausted.

Toxeus spoke first. 'The kill belongs to your nephew. You have done well.'

The others cheered.

'No uncle, you are wrong,' Meleager said and shook his head as he walked over to the boar's carcass. He gingerly placed his foot on the boar's head and turned to face the others. 'Atalanta's spear struck first. It was a fatal blow, and all I did was to merely finish-off the beast.'

'Hers was only a flesh wound!' Toxeus defended. 'She has no claim.'

'And I make no claim,' Atalanta yelled out.

'She has a claim to the kill because I say it is so!' Meleager was furious. His face flush with anger.

'Maybe she can be rewarded in some other way, for her taking first blood,' Jason suggested.

'Oh, you'd like that, wouldn't you friend?' Meleager yelled irrationally.

'If you deny yourself the kill, and the bitch makes no claim, then I can claim the pelt and tusks as my prize,' Toxeus boasted jovially. 'The prize is mine… and my brothers,' he declared and they laughed.

Meleager took this as further insult. He turned on his uncle and thrust his still bloodied sword into his uncle's chest, killing him instantly. As he fell to the ground, Plexippus charged Meleager with his own sword, but Meleager was younger and swifter, and he easily ducked away from the swords path. Meleager swung his sword and dealt a savage and fatal injury on the back of Plexippus neck as he moved past him.

Meleager now covered with blood, turned to the others. 'Is there anyone else?' he asked calmly.

No one spoke.

Meleager walked up to Atalanta. 'I claim you to be worthy of the prize. It was the wound that you inflicted that made all the difference.'

'I never wanted a reward or the trophy, Meleager. I only came here to help you because you were so kind to me about joining the Argo crew.' She smiled at him and he looked happy for it. 'This prize, and the love and respect that you'll receive from your people, are yours. I truly believe that you should claim it, and then revel in its glory!' she urged.

'I have strong feelings for you Atalanta,' Meleager told her as he looked at his feet.

She pulled his bloodied face up to meet hers. 'I know,' she replied. She was smiling happily. 'Let us conclude the hunt, return to the city, freshen up, celebrate, and then we can discuss our feelings for each other properly and in private.'

Meleager's heart leapt with joy in anticipation. Satisfied that there was no longer any threat, he warmly thanked each of the remaining hunters for their loyalty and service, and he promised them great rewards for bravery for their part in the hunt. He admitted he had made some mistakes, and he was clearly now attempting to win support for when the inevitable questions about human losses were accounted for. Most said nothing in response, which Meleager took to mean acquiescence.

Meleager had prepared a green flare which he now lit. It was to advise the runners that the boar was dead and that it was safe to come to their assistance. They slowly and cautiously drifted in, and they quietly set about the task of skinning the pelt, cutting the meat for the feast, and removing the tusks. The remainder would be left for scavengers to clean up. Both Castor and Polydeuces collected Toxeus and Plexippus bodies, and hefted them over a shoulder. Lynceus did the same for Mopsus. The three left the kill zone and headed off for the city followed by the others.

The victorious return of the hunters was highly anticipated. At the sight of the hunters, the citizens roared in happiness and they cheered as the city gates burst open and Calydonian's rushed out to assist the men who were burdened with dead warriors, boar meat, pelt, and the tusks of the now defeated beast.

OEneus and Althea rushed to their son and hugged him proudly. They were relieved at the success of the hunt and their son's safe return. Althea's joy soon turned to sadness when she saw the bodies of her two deceased brothers. She ordered her aids to take them to the surgeon to be examined but was immediately concerned when she could easily see that they were killed by men's weapons and not by an animal.

She confronted Meleager about the deaths of her brothers, but he was so self-absorbed by the people's praises, that he openly admitted to killing them. He looked at his mother shocked face and quickly added that his actions were only in self-defence over an ugly argument about the spoils. Althea was shocked, and so she retreated to her chambers to grieve and to think. At a private shrine to Artemis, she first gave her thanks for the death of the boar and for her son's safe return. She sat in muted silence, digesting her son's explanation. Next, she began sobbing in her grief for her beloved brothers. How could her son do this to them? No reason, however ugly, could give rise to murder. Meleager was her loving and devoted son and he was raised to be a future king. He had the respect of the people, and he had saved their kingdom from Artemis's demon monster. She loved him and yet, she hated him.

In a daze, Althea retrieved the sacred branch from its concealment. She slowly approached the fire, carefully unwrapping the branch from its cloth. She was willing it to give her some sign that she should return it to the hiding place, but she received none. The fire was freshly set alight by her staff and now burned fiercely. She hesitated before the flames as she shed tears for her contemplation and moral conflict. The Destinies had promised a swift death for her son, when the branch was reduced to dust. Her son was their legacy and represented the future of the kingdom, but her son had deliberately murdered her brothers and that was unforgivable.

Althea spoke barely above a whisper. 'Goddesses of punishment, behold the sacrifice I now deem to make to you. My husband OEneus rejoices his houses victory whilst the house of my father is desolate, and now mourns this grievous injustice. Do I plead for my departed brother's forgiveness as I spare my son, though he deserves death? If Meleager lives he will triumph, but my brothers will wander un-avenged amongst the shadows. Meleager lives only through my gift of life. He lived again when I saved him as a child. Now he wrongs me and it is his life that is mine to destroy and end forever. Die now Meleager, for your crimes.' Althea turned her face away from the flames but threw the branch into the fire. The wood immediately caught fire and in the intense heat it was quickly reduced to ash. Outside from the courtyard, there were screams of agony, and multiple shrieks of fear, which was followed by prolonged silence. She did not need to look outside her window, as she already knew that her son had died in agony.

Meleager's younger sisters wept uncontrollably for their brother's sudden death. He was their hero and the champion of Calydonia. Althea appealed to Artemis for assistance and the goddess arrived, having learned of all that had happened from Atalanta, she transformed the grieving sisters into birds and then she departed. Only Meleager's older sister, Deianeira survived, as she was abroad at the time. Althea couldn't reconcile her mixed grief for these recent tragedies. She drew her blade across her own throat and joined her son, and her brothers in the afterlife.

Days later, Iolaus, Castor, and Polydeuces sat at a public wine drinking establishment. They were now well away from the tragedies that would become famous as the misadventures of the Calydonian

Boar hunt. For their own part, they agreed that they had contributed little to either the beast's death, or to the tragic demise of their fellow hunters. Despite consuming much wine, they were yet to feel merry. 'I think Artemis was kind to all three of us,' Castor offered as his conclusion.

'We will be remembered for having been brave enough to have taken part in this hunt,' Iolaus said to the others. 'But I think our humble contribution of carrying the victims of this misadventure back to the city should be removed from any retelling of this story.'

Both Castor and Polydeuces nodded with their full agreement.

'Do you think if Herakles had been here, that it would have made a difference?' Polydeuces asked.

Iolaus snorted his laughter. 'No, no one could have foreseen or prevented this,' he replied. 'Besides, he has enough of his own tragedies without adding this one to his list.'

Both Castor and Polydeuces again nodded their agreement.

***

The ten-year war that had positioned Greeks against the Trojan's, had long term devastating consequences for both sides. They were once good friends, allies in conflicts, and strong trading partners. The war totally decimated the Trojans, their city in ruins, and the few survivors fled their once fabulous homeland to start new lives in faraway places. The surviving victorious Greeks also had many problems to deal with on their return to their homes, families, and kingdoms. The only positive was that through its actions, it had briefly united the Greeks as a nation.

Firstly, many of the Greek city kingdoms were financially ruined. The war had cost a great deal in human lives, equipment, and gold. Secondly, many of the warring kings were usurped during their absence. Whilst they were away, fighting for Greek honour, those who remained at home took advantage of the opportunities, and had seized control of their realm. Some kingdoms disappeared completely having been forcibly merged into neighbouring domains. Others had new kings and they quickly surrounded themselves with loyal men who were placed in positions of power and influence. Lastly, many of the surviving Greek warriors were disillusioned with the length, ferocity, and conclusion of the war. Many travelled to faraway lands to seek solace. Countless warriors laid down their weapons and searched to find some meaning to the war. Some just wanted to find a new home and a fresh beginning.

Many suffered guilt for their actions and what they had done to the Trojans. Numerous warriors never fully recovered from the physical or mental injuries, and some never returned to Greece.

Menelaus, who after the ten-year war with Troy was at last reunited with his wife Helen, had reluctantly forgiven her for her part in starting the conflict. Many Greeks believed she deserved a public brutal death for her betrayal of her husband and her many years of infidelity. As Menelaus chose not to take punitive action, they became angry, bitter, and very resentful.

It took many years for the two of them to return to Greece. They were constantly afflicted with heavy storms and head strong winds, that kept them away from home. Many people felt that it was the gods that were angry with them, and so they were kept away from Greece as punishment. They resolved to spend some time in Crete, and Menelaus was able to establish commerce with the local merchants. He did well and learned how to profit from the experience. He amassed a considerable fortune, but remained resolved to one day return to his home in Greece.

***

Ten years earlier, on the eve of the war, the goddess Artemis was offended when Agamemnon had publicly boasted that his hunting skills were better than hers. She punished him by stranding the entire Greek fleet with a strong and unrelenting westerly wind. To appease Artemis, Agamemnon offered their only daughter, Iphigenia, to be publicly put to death on a sacrificial alter in Artemis's honour. In this way he could start the war that he had promised to his brother, Menelaus, and the Greeks could commence fighting the Trojans for the return of Helen.

Iphigenia's mother Clytemnestra was devastated with his plan, and she pleaded for Artemis to explain to her the need to sacrifice her beloved daughter. Artemis took pity on the mother, and she told her that the sacrifice was symbolic of Agamemnon's apology, and that a deer would suffice. Agamemnon refused the change, claiming a daughter's sacrifice was more powerful than a deer, and so before a horrified audience, Iphigenia met her violent and bloodied fate.

Now, ten years later and at the conclusion of the war, Agamemnon returned home to discover he had a revengeful wife waiting for him. Clytemnestra, with her new lover Aegisthus, plotted his death for needlessly sacrificing her daughter. Aegisthus positioned himself as lookout watching for Agamemnon's ship to return to Argo. Agamemnon had sent word to Clytemnestra and asked that she prepared a warm bath, and a hero's banquet, for her returning victorious husband. Agamemnon was so pleased with her preparations that he immediately relaxed and enjoyed being safe in his own home. As he bathed, she threw a heavy robe over his face and proceeded to butcher him with an axe. She next ordered the execution of many of her husband's loyal officers, and also some of the new slaves who were former nobles of Troy. Clytemnestra was cunning enough to swifty remove any of the people who demonstrated loyalties to her former husband, and might choose to revenge him.

***

Both Castor and Polydeuces had fought as generals in the war, and they had led their fellow Spartan warriors well, losing only a few of them to the enemies' blade. They were able to win many of the battles that they fought in. During the campaign, they had agreed to a truce with their rival twin cousins Idas and Lynceus. They fought together against the Trojans and remained true to their warrior oaths, of watching each other's flanks and backs. Fortunately, both Castor and Polydeuces had remained unscathed. When the war was finally over, they could finally return home, to be reunited with their wives and their children. They returned to comfortable normal lives of teaching, training, and managing their cattle and horses.

After many years of peace, they received an invitation from their sister, Helen. They had returned to Greece and she was hosting a celebration of her husband's successes abroad. They were prosperous and wanted to share their happiness with family. Castor and Polydeuces also learned that both Idas and Lynceus would be there, and so they immediately set into action a plan that they had only previously dreamed of doing.

Melenaus was overt and pretentious about his successes abroad, and soon Idas and Lynceus were enthralled by him, and they greedily sought opportunity to bond with their uncle in any of his future enterprises. Whilst they were distracted, Castor and Polydeuces made simple excuses to leave the celebration, and they were casually dismissed. As soon as they left Melenaus' home they rushed for their horses and sped across the lands to Idas and Lynceus' cattle herds.

They planned to rustle them and merge them into their own herds as retribution for the cruel trick they had suffered when they were young men. Whilst their rivals were far away and were being entertained, wined, dined, and generally distracted, Castor and Polydeuces acted out their revenge.

When they arrived at the cattle yards, Castor climbed a tree in order to keep a lookout whilst Polydeuces expertly rounded up the cattle, and proceeded to herd them toward their new home. However, Idas and Lynceus were wary of their cousins. They didn't trust Castor and Polydeuces reasons for leaving the feast, and so they had immediately decided to follow them to learn what they were up to. It didn't take them long to realise that it was their cattle that they were stealing.

Lynceus's nickname was "the Lynx", for he had excellent night vision. He spotted Castor in the tree overlooking the herd of cattle.

'They are stealing our cattle,' Lynceus whispered with urgency to Idas.

'We'll stop them and make an example of them,' Idas replied. They motioned their horses to speed up and they raced to try to prevent the theft of their cattle.

As they rushed to the tree, Castor yelled the warning to his brother. As Castor was descending the tree, Idas, furious for their act of thievery, thrust his spear into Castors side, inflicting in him a fatal wound. Polydeuces rushed back and was now near to his brother and he thrust his sword, stabbing Idas in the neck, spewing out a geyser of blood. Idas fell dead in front of his brother Lynceus, who dismounted and was about to spear Polydeuces in the chest when a massive lightning bolt struck Lynceus, incinerating him where he stood. The roar of thunder quickly followed.

As the dawn sky approached, Polydeuces looked about him to see if he could find the source of the lightening. There, on top of the hill, stood his father, Zeus. Zeus walked toward the now distraught Polydeuces. His twin brother was dying and he looked into Zeus' eyes and begged. 'Please save him o great father,' Polydeuces pleaded.

Zeus knelt down and examined the profusely bleeding Castor. 'His wound is fatal,' Zeus concluded.

'Will you please save him?' Polydeuces implored.

Zeus smiled. He hadn't asked, "Could he save him", he had just asked him to "save him." 'I can, but I know you are both guilty of attempting to steal other men's cattle.' Zeus admonished. He looked at Polydeuces and could see the shame on the man's face.

'It was only in revenge for a previous theft that they had done to us...' Polydeuces tried desperately to explain.

'I know you have both done many brave deeds during your life time,' Zeus smiled benevolently.

'We have...' Polydeuces started to agree, but his voice trailed off.

'I will grant you immortality and you can live with me at Mount Olympus,' Zeus offered. 'You are my son and you have proven yourself worthy.'

'But, what about my brother?'

'His fate is with Hades,' Zeus looked solemn as he broke the news.

'Isn't there something I can do?' Polydeuces asked hopefully. 'We have never been apart,' he explained.

Zeus could see the pain of imminent loss and separation on his son's face and he sympathised. 'You could agree to share your immortality,' he suggested.

'Yes! Yes!' Polydeuces quickly agreed without understanding what all that was implied.

'It would mean that for part of your time, you'd both enjoy the luxuries of Mount Olympus, but both of you would also have to spend an equal amount of time serving my brother, Hades.'

'I accept.' Polydeuces knelt before his brother. Before his eyes the wound closed and his breathing returned to normal. The spilled blood dried and blew away in the gentle breeze. Castor smiled at his brother. Polydeuces smiled at Zeus in his appreciation.

Zeus was so moved by Polydeuces selfless act to save his brother, that he commemorated them with two stars in the heavens. They were the two very bright stars they called "The Twins", and soon those stars became the two brightest stars in what is known to us as the constellation Gemini.

***

$$7$$

# *Novella one - the constellation Pisces*

Also, by Stephan De Jonghe

**The "Greek Constellations" series of novellas.**

The ancient Greeks identified and named Forty-Eight out of the Eighty-Eight recognised constellations. They were catalogued by a Greek astronomer Claudius Ptolemy in his publication the Almagest around 150 CE. The origins of the mythological stories that identified the constellations predate this documentation by as much as a thousand years.

**Novella one - the constellation Pisces and the story of Aphrodite and Eros, the Two Fishes.**

Aphrodite is well known as the Greek goddess of love, romance, and sexuality. Aphrodite is also known to us as   Venus, and the planet is named after her in her  honour. This is the story of how Aphrodite came to be. Born in the ocean during a struggle between father and son, she was raised on an island.

As an adult she was carried by Zeus to Mount Olympus to work and play with the gods and goddesses who resided there.

After a brief marriage to Hephaestus, she formed a steamy relationship with Hephaestus's brother, Ares and they had a son they named Eros. All her life, she struggled with the  unwanted, yet amorous advances of the Titan monster named, Typhon. Eventually, she and Eros had to flee Mount Olympus to escape his wrath, and they eventually became the constellation of the Two Fishes, known to us as Pisces.

**This book is now also available as an eBook**

Visit my website <u>www.folliclefarm.com.au</u> to learn more, or to purchase your paperback copy.

# 8

# *Novella two – the constellation of Capricorn*

ovella two – the constellation of Capricorn and the story of Pricus the Sea-Goat.

Pricus is an old sea-goat with a problem. He is regarded as the old man of the sea. The younger generation wants desperately to abandon the old ways, and leave their ocean home to live a more adventurous life on the land. The sea-goats are able to morph from sea-goats into land goats when they emerge from the surf to walk on land. They quickly learn to morph into human form, and to their delight discover that they can have much more fun exploring the plethora of opportunities that await them. In their naivety they make many mistakes, some ending in tragedy. Pricus is desperate to save the younger generation from themselves, and so must become increasingly resourceful do so, and do so in a way that his solution remains permanent. His dedication to his own kind earns him his place as the constellation of the sea-goat, known to us as Capricornus or Capricorn.

**Planned launch 2026**

# 9

# Novella three - Saturn's moon

Novella three - Saturn's moon Pandora and the story of the first human woman.

Zeus, king of the Greek God's, commissioned his son Hephaestus to craft the first human woman. Aided by Athena, he  carefully researched the perfect form and then moulded her from clay He then painted and glazed her into the perfect  woman. After being fired in his kiln, she was given the breath of life by the wind god Zephyr. She was named Pandora, being the bearer of the gifts  bequeathed to her by the gods and goddesses of Mount Olympus. Her main purpose for humanity was to become the role model for all future human women. Zeus then commanded that she be properly trained so that she can navigate life's complexities, but her tutors do too good a job with her, and she becomes too powerful for a normal human life. Zeus became disillusioned with her, and he decided that she should be married off to a minor god, so that she'll do no harm to herself, or to others.

Pandora's story is so significant that she is honoured as Pandora, one of Saturn's moons.

**This book is now also available as an eBook**

Visit my website www.folliclefarm.com.au to learn more, or to purchase your paperback copy.

**10**

# Novella four - the constellation Taurus

**N**ovella four - the constellation Taurus and the story of the Jupiter's moon Europa and her meeting with the white bull.

When Zeus, king and master of the gods and goddesses of Mount Olympus finds himself between wives he sets out on a desperate search for the perfect woman to marry. On a sunny field, set amongst spring flowers, on a stretch of land adjacent to the sea, he finds her. She is Europa, a gorgeous African princess. For Zeus, it becomes love at first sight. In his infatuation for this woman, he tries numerous times to impress her, and he almost succeeds. Sadly, for Zeus, his one true love is betrothed to another, and sadly for Zeus, a daughter must do her duty. Disguised as a magnificent white bull, he tries one last desperate attempt to have her.

The consequences of his quest for true love are celebrated as the constellation of the white bull, know to us as the Taurus.

Also commemorated in this story is the constellation Draco, known as Ladon the Dragon. Also featured is Laelaps as the constellation Canis Major or Greater Dog, and the Teumessian Fox as the constellation Canis Minor or Lesser Dog.

**Planned launch 2025**

# 11

# Novella five - the constellations Scorpio & Orion

N ovella five - the constellations Scorpio & Orion and the story of the scorpion verses the hunter.

Artemis is the goddess of the forests and of the hunt. She befriends a hunter named Orion. Their friendship is slowly progressing toward a blossoming romance when Orion boasts of his ability to wantonly kill all the animals that cross his path. Artemis is dismayed. Her policy is to only kill for food, to kill for pleasure is an outrage. She feels she must sacrifice her future relationship by stopping Orion from completing his boast. She manifests a giant scorpion and sends it to attack and destroy Orion. A massive battle ensues and both are defeated, thus preserving animal life from indiscriminate killings. To celebrate the outcome and to remind us that all life is precious, their images are cast into the heavens as the constellation *Orion* and the constellation of the Scorpion known to us as *Scorpio*.

**Planned launch 2025**

**12**

# *Novella six - the constellation Aries*

**N**ovella six - the constellation Aries and the story of Chrysomallos the Ram.

Born from a union between Poseidon and Theophane on a remote island that was the home of a flock of sheep. They are interrupted by shepherds during copulation, so they disguised themselves as sheep to avoid the embarrassment that Theophane might suffer if their tryst became public knowledge. Their male child is born with the ability to morph from human form into a ram. From his father, he has long golden hair, and when he becomes a ram, he has golden fleece. He has wings and the ability to fly.

He is raised by his loving mother, Theophane and is named Chrysomallos. He eventually befriends the prince Phrixus and princess Helle who live in a nearby kingdom. When their lives become perilous, Chrysomallos the flying, golden fleeced Ram, comes to their rescue. His bravery is celebrated as the constellation of the Ram, know to us as *Aries*.

**Planned launch 2024**

13

# *Novella seven - the constellation of Ophiuchus*

**N**ovella seven - the constellation of Ophiuchus and the story of Asclepius the serpentius or serpent bearer.

Asclepius was the son of Apollo. When Apollo had to rescue Asclepius from his dying mother's womb, he realised that he didn't know enough about medicine and surgery, and so he set about discovering as much as he could. He later taught all that he learned to his son. Next, to further his education, Apollo decided that Asclepius would learn even more from the tutor Chiron. Through him he completed his training, and went on to be the foremost authority on how to manage illness and repair injuries. His wife Epione and he had five daughters and three sons, and all became involved in the practice of medical treatments.

Their most prominent daughter was Hygieia and the practice of hygiene is named after her.

Both Apollo and Asclepius have been forever revered as the fathers of medical treatments and their names were included in the original Hippocratic Oath, that all medical practitioners swore upon when becoming formally registered to become doctors.

His dedication to healing the sick and injured was commemorated in the night sky as the constellation *Ophiuchus*. Many people who practice in astrology believe that Ophiuchus is the unrecognised thirteenth star sign.

Also featured is the constellation of *Serpens* or "The Snake." Who Asclepius witnessed bringing healing herbs to another snake who was sick, and this event started him on his discovery of benefits of medicinal herbs.

**Planned launch 2026**

# 14

# Novella eight - the constellations of Cancer & Leo

**N**ovella eight - the constellations of Cancer & Leo and the stories of Karkinos the giant crab, Zosma the Nemean lioness, Astron the hydra, Aquila the eagle, Sagitta the arrow, and the constellation named after Herakles the Demi-God.

The birth of Herakles was surrounded by controversy. Being the demi-god son of the King of all the gods, he found it difficult to live a routine life with his wife and children.

Herakles was persecuted by Hera for being her husband Zeus's illegitimate son, and so he was inflicted by incessant painful headaches. He was told of a remedy by the oracle in Delphi, but before he could be cured, it required him to agree to take on many incredible tasks which were assigned to him by the local king.

By completing these labours, he should be able to go on to live a long and fulfilling life.

He later became immortal and Herakles is forever remembered as a Greek Mythological hero for defeating the giant crab that became known as constellation Cancer. He also killed the man-eating lioness that became known as the constellation Leo. He slew the serpent of Lake Lerna, which is now known as the constellation Hydra. Herakles used an arrow now known as the constellation Sagitta to kill a giant eagle that became to be known as the constellation Aquila or "The Eagle".

Herakles was finally accepted at Mount Olympus and was honoured with the constellation Herakles also known as Hercules.

**This book is now also available as an eBook**

Visit my website www.folliclefarm.com.au to learn more, or to purchase your paperback copy.

15

# *Novella nine - the constellation Gemini*

Novella nine - the constellation Gemini and the story of the twins, Castor and Polydeuces.

Leucippe was desperate to become a grandmother. Fed up with her son-in-law's lack of progress, she asked Zeus for help. When Zeus arrived, he took the opportunity, disguised himself as a swan, and then he did much more than just arrange for Leda to become pregnant.

The Spartan twins grew up to become skilled horsemen, hunters, warriors, and adventurers. They embarked on many journeys together and their adventures included sailing on the Argo with Jason on his quest for the golden fleece, being hunters at the Calydonian wild boar hunt, and fighting Trojans at Troy. It was their sister Helen, who was the central reason for that protracted war.

The twins were honoured by Zeus for their bravery and commitment to each other, and he cast their image into the night sky to be forever remembered as the constellation of the Twins, which is now known as *Gemini.*

143

Also featured in this story is the constellation The Swan or *Cygnus*.

**This book is now also available as an eBook**

Visit my website www.folliclefarm.com.au to learn more, or to purchase your paperback copy.

16

# *Novella ten - the constellations of Virgo & Libra*

**N**ovella ten - the constellations of Virgo & Libra and the story of the Astraea the maiden and Themis the scales.

Astraea and Themis were both goddesses who were committed to advancing the living conditions of the humans who lived on the island of Thera. Along with other gods and goddess they believed that they'd become the role models for all future human progress advancements.

Astraea strongly believed in justice and sort punishment for those that transgressed against the common good. Her belief was that punishment was a deterrent and that the formal process of trial and conviction for those found guilty of a crime had a place in society.

Themis was more about bringing about restitution to an aggrieved person who was treated unfairly by another. He mediation skills gave rise to the belief that there was always a remedy when agreements fell apart.

145

However, the speed of their progress and their intentions to achieve self-determination worried Zeus. After inspecting the work and assessing all that had been achieved, he concluded that it must come to an abrupt end. And as every Greek immortal knows, when Zeus is determined and has made up his mind, nothing stops it his decision from happening. For Astraea the decision was devastating, so she cast herself into the night sky as "the maiden", forever watching over humanity as the constellation **Virgo**.

Themis was later honoured for her balanced outlook on life, and is remembered as the scales as she evenly balanced out her reasoning and decisions. She is now known to us as the constellation **Libra**.

**Planned launch 2025**

# 17

# *Novella eleven – the constellation Aquarius*

Novella eleven – the constellation Aquarius and the story of Ganymede the water bearer.

Ganymede was adopted by a family of shepherds when he was found abandoned as a young child. He preferred his own company, and whilst good at caring for the sheep he was regarded as a misfit by his adopted family.

One day, as he tending the sheep, he was spotted by Zeus, who flying past in his eagle form. Out of curiosity Zeus landed to meet the young man and became quickly enamoured with him. Ganymede found himself attracted to the powerful God and very much wanted to be with him. Zeus easily convinced the young man to give up his shepherding life and come with him to Mount Olympus.

Ganymede became Zeus's friend and lover. He took over the role of cup bearer during important civil functions from Zeus's daughter Hebe, as she had found love and married a Greek Hero.

Ganymede quickly became fascinated with aqueducts and fountains, and he was responsible for improving the water quality and availability of clean drinking water to Mount Olympus's inhabitants. His contribution is celebrated as the constellation of the "water bearer" now know to us as **Aquarius.**

**Planned launch 2025**

# 18

# *Novella twelve – the constellation of Sagittarius*

**N**ovella twelve – the constellation of Sagittarius and the story of the "Archer" Crotus.

A water Naiad nymph named Eupheme was a demi-goddess of the Hippocrene freshwater spring near Mount Helicon. She was youthful, very beautiful, and  powerful.  She met and had a relationship with the God Pan, a Satyr, famous for playing the pipes was the god of shepherds, flocks, rustic musicians, and improvisation. Their romance led to the birth of Crotus.

Crotus was a Satyr and grew up to be like his like his father, preferring the company of muses. Most Satyrs preferred the company of Dionysus, God of wine, revelry, and debauchery, so Crotus was unusual in this way.

The muses were providers of inspiration to artists, musicians, poets, story tellers, artisans, entertainers, and dancers. They brought out the natural talents of those they inspired, and positively encouraged them to excel by pursuing their passions and striving for perfection in their chosen art form.

Crotus was also a great hunter and many say that he invented the hunting bow. He was more popular as a musician and his most noteworthy contribution to performance music was the addition of rhythmic beats used to accompany the musician's musical score. He was also responsible for the introduction of a ritual applause to signify both pleasure from the performance and gratitude to the artist for their dedication to the composition and the quality of the performance. The applause was widely recognised as a significant motivator for artistic excellence.

Crotus was a mortal, and when he died, the Younger Muses petitioned Zeus to have his likeness immortalised as place in the night sky. Their petition was positively received and, in his honour, he created the constellation of the Archer which is known to us as **Sagittarius**.

**Planned launch 2026**

# 19

# Novella thirteen – the constellation Centaurus

Novella thirteen – the constellation Centaurus and the story of the tutor Cheiron.

Cheiron was a centaur who became the tutor to many of the legendary heroes of Greek mythology. Unlike other centaurs, Cheiron was intelligent, civilised and very kind. He was the teacher of students that included Jason, Castor, Polydeuces, Asclepius, Peleus, and Achilles and he taught them philosophy, archery, hunting, medicine, music, gymnastics, and the art of prophecy.

His life ended tragically when he was accidentally struck with a poisoned arrow by his close friend, Herakles. Herakles had loosed the arrow in an attempt to ward off marauding cruel centaurs who came to cause mischief to Cheiron, but in the confusion, Cheiron stepped into the path of the arrow and was stuck. His immortality prevented his death, but the strong poison caused him everlasting agony.

He decided to surrender his immortality to Zeus so that he could pass into the underworld. He was then commemorated as the constellation of the Centaur and is known to us as **Centaurus.**

**Planned launch 2025**

**The other Greek constellations** that are yet to be featured in this series include Andromeda, Ara, Auriga, Boötes, Cassiopeia, Cepheus, Corona Australis, Corona Borealis, Corvus, Crater, Delphinus, Equuleus, Eridanus, Lepus, Lupus, Lyra, Pegasus, Perseus, Piscis, Austrinus, Triangulum, Ursa Major, Ursa Minor, and Argo Navis (now divided into Carina, Puppis, and Vela)

# 20

# Follicle Farm – A novel adventure

**O**ther books available by Stephan De Jonghe

**Follicle Farm – A novel adventure. (Fiction)**

Follicle Farm is a comical and imaginative insight into organisational structure and behaviour of the trillions of cells that make up the microscopic world of every living person. It reveals how cells within the human body really think and how they, mostly, work well together. Bobby is a Mitochondria and he works as a humble Follicle Farmer. He, with millions of colleagues, are part of the amazing organisation dedicated to growing hair for the human male that they live inside of. Recently, Bobby made an important discovery when he learned how to reverse the effects of alopecia and greying hair. Now it's up to management to debate if they should use his technique.

Join Bobby as he travels the body, ably assisted by Banjo and Skip, as he meets and deals with other human cells in various systems throughout the body. Bobby quickly learns there is more to management than just servicing the body's needs. Cliques, quirks, politics, unions, and hidden agendas, all thrive in Bobby's world.

You'll share in his adventure of personal growth as he encourages other Follicle Farmers to utilise best practises in growing quality hair.

**This book is now available in Paperback or eBook**

Visit my website <u>www.folliclefarm.com.au</u> to learn more, or to purchase your paperback copy.

**21**

# *Your concise guide to the meaning of life*

**Y**our concise guide to the meaning of life. (Non-Fiction)

This is a serious book designed to help people. Its main purpose is to assist you on how to gain insights on how to live a happier and more fulfilled life. It will give the you, the reader, instant benefits. It is peppered with many great quotes, many of them are my own. I've combined my interest in philosophy, sociology, psychology, and history to delve into the true meaning of life. The reader will not only understand why they are here, but how to make their experience more meaningful.

My main aim is to inspire readers into taking more control of how they make decisions that positively affect their achievements, successes, happiness, and therefore their well-being. The book is a summary of concise points that are easy to learn and apply to the readers life for an immediate benefit. It includes popular relevant quotes to re-enforce the messages and teaching. I have also included personal anecdotes that give real life and meaningful examples of how the material applies to all readers.

155

Topics include

- an explanation the main purpose for living.
- how to improve your relationships.
- how communication works and how to make it more effective.
- understanding your needs and desires and how to improve outcomes for yourself.
- understanding what motivates other people.
- how to exceed your own expectations.
- understanding your own personal legal, moral, ethical, and value system.
- improving your control over your emotions.
- understanding the concepts of faith, fate and fairness.
- and being better prepared for the final stages of your life.

**This book is now available in Paperback or eBook**

Visit the website <u>www.folliclefarm.com.au</u> to learn more, or to purchase your paperback copy.